**Two sisters can get into more
trouble than one!
Two sisters . . . one city . . .
big trouble!**

STEPHANIE

"Oh, one more thing," Danny Tanner added. "Stephanie, you're in charge. Michelle, listen to your sister. Do what she tells you. And have fun!"

Fun? Stephanie thought. *I'm in the most exciting city in the world. And I'm supposed to hang out with my little sister!* She glanced over at Michelle and shook her head.

Did I really fly all the way to New York just to baby-sit? she wondered. *How could that be?*

MICHELLE

Michelle hesitated. She couldn't tell Kaye she was stuck in the hotel—doing nothing, while her big sister *baby-sat* her!

Kaye's mother, Mrs. Bloom, smiled at Michelle. "Maybe you should come with us to FAO Schwarz."

Michelle's heart leapt. "That would be fantastic," she said. "But . . . uh, I don't know if—"

"You don't know if your big sister will let you, do you?" Kaye asked.

Michelle straightened her shoulders. "I told you, I can do what I want!"

This was turning into a great day after all!

FULL HOUSE™: SISTERS books

Two on the Town

One Boss Two Many
(coming in mid-December 1999)

Available from MINSTREL Books

FULL HOUSE™
SISTERS

Two on
the Town

Devra Newberger Speregen

A Parachute Book

Published by POCKET BOOKS
New York   London   Toronto   Sydney   Tokyo   Singapore

A MINSTREL PAPERBACK *Original*

 A Minstrel Book published by
POCKET BOOKS, a division of Simon & Schuster Inc.
1230 Avenue of the Americas, New York, NY 10020

A PARACHUTE BOOK

 Copyright © and ™ 1998 by Warner Bros.

ISBN: 0-671-02149-4

First Minstrel Books printing November 1998

10 9 8 7 6 5 4 3 2 1

A MINSTREL BOOK and colophon are registered trademarks of Simon & Schuster Inc.

Cover photo by Schultz Photography

Printed in the U.S.A.

Two on the Town

Chapter
1

"We're really in New York City!" Stephanie Tanner exclaimed. She dropped her suitcase on one of the two king-size beds. Then she turned to her ten-year-old sister, Michelle.

"Can you believe the size of this hotel room?" Stephanie asked. "We could fit our bedroom *and* D.J.'s in here!"

D.J. was their nineteen-year-old sister.

"I know." Michelle spread her arms out and spun around. "I feel like I'm in a palace!"

Stephanie grinned. "It's not *that* grand. But it is pretty amazing to have all this space to ourselves."

1

Back in San Francisco, Stephanie and Michelle shared a bedroom. They also shared their house with their dad, D.J., their uncle Jesse, his wife, Becky, and their five-year-old twins, their dad's good friend, Joey—and the dog, Comet.

"Four days in a luxury hotel in New York City," Stephanie said. "It's like a dream come true."

"It *is* a dream," Michelle told her. "We're missing two whole days of *school* for this trip!"

Stephanie examined the packet of hotel stationery on the desk. "The Windsor" was written across the top in elegant gold letters. "Who would have thought that Dad would actually let us take a four-day weekend?" she said.

"That's because we both did so brilliantly at school," Michelle reminded her. The trip was a reward. Their dad promised to take Stephanie and Michelle to New York if they both improved their math grades.

Stephanie rolled her eyes and shook her long, blond hair back from her face. "I can't

2

believe how much time I spent doing word problems. But it was worth it!"

"Even though our teachers said we have to make up any work we miss," Michelle added.

"Right," Stephanie said. "So I'm not going to waste a minute of my time here. I'm going to have a ton of fun, every second!"

"Steph, look at this!" Michelle poked her head into the bathroom. "My hair looks extra blond in this mirror!"

Stephanie stepped in beside Michelle and peeked into the mirror. "Maybe that's because the mirror is framed in gold!"

"The sinks are gold, too," Michelle pointed out. "And we have *two* of them, all to ourselves. And there's a phone in here, and this gigantic, funny-looking bathtub."

"That's not just a bathtub. It's a Jacuzzi," Stephanie explained. "A bathtub with a built-in whirlpool. The water gives you a massage."

"Wow!" Michelle stepped out of the bathroom and examined the rest of the room. "And there's a wide-screen TV, and our own refrigerator! And little chocolate mints on the pillows!"

Stephanie opened the heavy brocade drapes. She gazed out the window. Their room was on the fortieth floor. The people walking on the sidewalk seemed tiny.

"Look at this view, Michelle," Stephanie said. "You can practically see all of New York City. Now, *that's* incredible!"

She pointed straight ahead to a large area of trees. "That must be Central Park." A cluster of brightly colored rooftops showed through a clearing in the trees. "And I bet that's the Central Park Zoo."

"Where?" Michelle rushed to the window. "I can't wait to go to the zoo!" she said. "I promised to take a photograph of Ling-Ling and Tsing-Tsing for my class."

Ling-Ling and Tsing-Tsing were famous Chinese pandas. They were on loan to the Central Park Zoo this month. Michelle's fourth-grade class at home was learning all about China. They were excited that Michelle might see the pandas.

"I'm sure we'll get to the zoo—sometime," Stephanie said.

4

"Sometime? Why can't we go there first?" Michelle asked.

"Because this is my first time ever in New York City. I have better things to do than go to the zoo," Stephanie replied.

"Well, it's my first time, too," Michelle argued. "Besides, nothing is better than the zoo."

"Well, I'm oldest. And oldest gets to pick first," Stephanie declared.

"No way!" Michelle protested. "You got to sit by the window on the airplane. So I should get first pick."

"Forget it, Michelle!" Stephanie's voice rose. "You said you *wanted* the middle seat, next to Dad. So now I get first pick!"

"That is so unfair!" Michelle protested. "I wish Dad just took *me* to New York. Then I could do whatever I wanted."

"Well, I wish the same thing," Stephanie shot back. "Because I'm not going to waste four whole days arguing with you."

Stephanie pulled a list out of her shoulder bag. One of her best friends back home, Allie Taylor, had visited New York last spring.

5

Allie had given Stephanie a list of cool places to see.

"Okay, our first stop will be the Hard Rock Cafe," Stephanie read from the list. "Then we'll take the ferry to the Statue of Liberty. Or maybe we'll get tickets to a Broadway show first. Or—"

"What about the Empire State Building?" Michelle interrupted. "And Fifth Avenue! I told Cassie and Mandy you'd take a picture of me strolling on Fifth Avenue, like a real celebrity."

"Michelle, it's no big deal to walk on Fifth Avenue. Besides, it's right below our window!"

"It is? Then let's go!" Michelle exclaimed.

"Hold it!" Danny Tanner appeared in a doorway across the room.

"Dad! Why were you in our closet?" Michelle asked.

Danny laughed. "Michelle, this isn't a closet," he explained. "It's the door to *my* room. I asked for connecting rooms, remember?"

"Oh! Right," Michelle said.

"So, how's the unpacking going?" Danny asked.

"Forget unpacking," Stephanie said. "Let's go get tickets to a Broadway show. What should it be? *The Sound of Music, Cats, Phantom of the Opera?*"

Danny put a hand on Stephanie's shoulder. "I'm sorry, sweetheart. We can't do that today," he said.

Stephanie stared at him in shock. "We can't?" she asked.

"Great!" Michelle declared. "Then let's head straight to the Central Park Zoo. It's so close, you can see it from our window. Can we? Please?"

"No way!" Stephanie shouted. "We'll go to the Hard Rock Cafe for an early lunch!"

"Yuck!" Michelle exclaimed. "Why should we do what *you* want to do?"

"Why should we do what *you* want to do?" Stephanie countered.

Danny held up his hands. "Stop arguing!" he exclaimed. "I'll settle this. We're *not* going to the zoo today."

"But, Dad!" Michelle wailed.

"And we're not going to a show or a res-taurant, either," Danny went on.

"Dad! That's not fair—" Stephanie began.

Danny held up his hands again. "Whoa! Hold on," he said. "The reason we're not going to those places *today* is because I have to *work* today. Don't forget, I came to New York for a business trip."

Danny and their aunt Becky co-hosted a morning TV show called *Wake Up, San Francisco*. He was in New York to interview a guest who couldn't fly to the West Coast.

"I brought you girls along because I thought you'd enjoy it," he went on. "Not to spend it fighting!"

"We can't help it, Dad," Stephanie told him. "We're just so excited about seeing the city. We can't wait to get started."

"And we *will* see the sights," Danny promised. "Tomorrow."

"But what are *we* supposed to do today?" Stephanie asked. She glanced at her watch. "It's only eleven in the morning. We can't waste an entire day!"

"You'll stay here in the hotel room," her

8

father replied. "Until I'm through with work."

"Dad! You can't mean that!" Stephanie exclaimed in horror. "We can't do *anything* at all?"

Danny ran a hand through his wavy, black hair. "Well, I suppose it would be okay for you to leave the room," he said. "As long as you stay together," he added.

Stephanie brightened. "Okay! We promise!" she said.

"And stay in the hotel," Danny added.

"In the hotel?" Stephanie stared at him in disbelief. "What could we do in the hotel?"

"Can't we even take a walk?" Michelle asked. "Just around the block, to check out the zoo? It's practically right across the street!"

"Sorry." Danny shook his head as he put on his coat. His voice was stern. "You don't know your way around New York City," he said. "And you have no idea how easy it is to get lost in a big city. You're not responsible enough to be on your own."

"Well, I am!" Stephanie exclaimed. "Dad, I'm fourteen," she reminded him. "I get around by myself at home, all the time. And San Francisco is a pretty big city, too!"

"And I'm responsible, too," Michelle insisted. "Don't treat me like a baby."

"Sorry, girls. No arguments." Danny's expression softened. "Hey, it's only for a few hours," he said. "I'll be back by four o'clock. *Then* we'll start the fun. I *promise!* We'll go wherever you want." He bent and gave Stephanie and Michelle each a kiss on the forehead.

"Here." He gave them each a twenty-dollar bill. "There are lots of shops and a restaurant off the lobby. You can get yourself some lunch downstairs. And just so there are no mix-ups—"

Danny picked up the packet of stationery on the desk. Included with the paper were envelopes and the Windsor's business cards. Danny took out two of the cards. On each one he wrote their room number, 4014.

"Just so neither one of you forgets," he said. He handed each girl a card. "Oh, one more thing," he added. "Stephanie, you're in charge. Michelle, listen to your sister. Do what she tells you."

"Dad!" Michelle protested. "I didn't come to New York so I could be bossed around!"

"Just stick together," Danny said. He waved as he left the room. "See you both later. And have fun!"

Fun? Stephanie thought. *I'm in the most exciting city in the world. And I'm supposed to hang out with my little sister!* She glanced over at Michelle.

Michelle was pulling clothes and toys out of her suitcase. They already covered her bed and were tumbling onto the floor.

Stephanie shook her head. *Did I really fly all the way to New York just to baby-sit?* she wondered. *How could that be?*

Chapter
2

Stephanie glared at Michelle.

"Don't look at me that way," Michelle told her. "It's not my fault. Do you think I want to be stuck here with *you?*" She flopped onto the bed. "I want to do something fun!"

"You're right. It's not your fault," Stephanie agreed. She glanced at her watch again. "But this is a total drag. I mean, it's only eleven o'clock in the morning. Five whole hours with nothing to do!" she groaned. "This is *not* how I pictured our big New York vacation!"

"I guess we could watch TV," Michelle

1 2

said. "Don't they show good movies in hotel rooms?"

"Let's see," Stephanie replied. She picked up the listings from the top of the television set. "We already saw all the good movies," she told Michelle. "And the best TV shows don't start until the afternoon."

"So much for fun in the big city," Michelle said.

She looked so miserable that Stephanie felt sorry for her.

"Hey, what's wrong with us?" Stephanie said. "We shouldn't be upset. I mean, look on the bright side. Dad left us on our *own!* That's fun, right?"

"It is?" Michelle asked.

"Sure," Stephanie told her. "I mean, we can't go outside. But we still have this whole big, fancy hotel to hang out in!"

She forced a smile, trying to cheer them *both* up. "We could go explore the shops in the lobby."

"Yeah," Michelle said, starting to get into it. "I saw signs for a game room downstairs. That might be fun."

"The game room?" Stephanie frowned.

Playing dumb video arcade games was *not* her idea of major fun. But their dad said they had to stick together.

"Well, we could do a little of that," Stephanie said. "But then it's my turn to pick what we do."

"What do you want to do?" Michelle asked.

Stephanie needed ideas. She noticed a big, shiny magazine on her bedside table. It was called *Windsor Adventures.*

"Hey, let me check this out. It lists all kinds of exciting things here in the hotel." Stephanie flipped through the pages.

"Michelle—look!" she cried in excitement. She showed her a full-page color photo.

"It's Sabrina!" Michelle exclaimed. "She's my most favorite teen model in the whole world!"

"Mine, too," Stephanie agreed. "And it says in this article that Sabrina stayed right here at the Windsor hotel! Just like us!"

Michelle squinted at her. "You know, you kind of look like Sabrina. If you changed your hair and wore different makeup. And wore better clothes," she added.

"Thanks for the compliment, Michelle," Stephanie said, rolling her eyes.

"No, I meant that in a nice way," Michelle insisted. "Why don't you do your hair like Sabrina's?"

"You mean, put it in a French twist, and leave one strand dangling over my left eye?" Stephanie shook her head. "I don't think so. It would look dumb on me."

"Why?" Michelle asked. "You don't think it looks dumb on Sabrina. I bet you'd look great!"

"Do you really think so?" Stephanie moved to the mirror, lifted her long, blond hair off her neck, and squinted. She *did* look like Sabrina!

"You know, I packed all my best clothes for this trip," Stephanie said. "And I borrowed one really great outfit from D.J."

D.J. was in college. She couldn't come on the trip because she was busy writing a paper. So she had to stay home with the rest of the family.

Michelle giggled at Stephanie's reflection in the mirror. "With D.J.'s clothes, you'd really look like Sabrina," she said. "I mean, people who don't know you might actually think you're her!"

"Really?" Stephanie asked. But she had to admit she looked much more sophisticated with her hair up that way.

Suddenly, Stephanie got an idea. Not just any idea—the best idea ever. For the next four days she was going to give herself a new identity. She wouldn't be plain, ordinary Stephanie Tanner from San Francisco anymore.

She'd be totally cool. Totally hip. Totally sophisticated. Totally New York! She would even call herself Sabrina.

With their dad gone for the afternoon, 'Sabrina' could check out the hotel. And maybe find some ultra-cute New York guys.

Michelle bounced on the end of her bed. "Can we go down to the lobby right now?"

"As soon as we unpack—and find the right clothes to wear," Stephanie answered.

She lifted her suitcase onto the bed and popped it open. She carefully lifted out a pair of slinky black bell-bottom pants.

"Hey, are those D.J.'s?" Michelle asked.

"Yeah. Aren't they cool?" Stephanie said.

She glanced at Michelle's pink overalls and bright purple T-shirt. "Uh, Michelle," she said. "Don't you want to change clothes, too?"

"Why should I?" Michelle asked. "I like this outfit."

"It's cute," Stephanie admitted, "but you've been wearing it for two days."

"No, I haven't," Michelle argued. "I put these overalls on right before we left for the airport."

"But we flew *overnight*," Stephanie pointed out. "That means you put them on *yesterday*. And they look it."

Michelle sighed. "Okay, okay, I'll change. But then can we go to the lobby? I want to find that chocolate shop."

"You mean the one we saw when Dad checked us into the hotel?" Stephanie asked.

"Right," Michelle answered. "I saw chocolate racing cars in the window! Nicky and Alex would love them."

Stephanie nodded. Their five-year-old twin cousins *would* love racing cars made out of chocolate. But cool, hip Sabrina wouldn't be very interested in candy.

Michelle quickly pulled on a white over-sized sweatshirt and black leggings. "Ready! Come on, Stephanie," she called.

"Wait a minute," Stephanie replied. "I'm having a fashion crisis! I forgot to pack the black clogs that go with D.J.'s bell-bottoms! The only shoes I have are brown flats and my white sneakers. Well, actually, I have my dress shoes, but they don't go at all!"

Michelle rolled her eyes and groaned. "Just pick something," she said.

"I can't. Sabrina—I mean, *I* want to look just right," Stephanie said.

She glanced at herself in the dresser mirror again.

"Yikes!" One side of her hair was all squished down from where she'd leaned against her seat on the plane.

"Oh, no!" Stephanie exclaimed. "I have airplane hair! I can't let anyone see me like this! I'd better shampoo it and blow it dry again."

"But that will take forever," Michelle complained.

"I know." Stephanie hesitated. It wasn't

18

fair to ask Michelle to wait for her to shower
and change. On the other hand, there was no
way she could walk out of their room looking like this. Maybe if she really hurried . . .

"Listen, Michelle," Stephanie said. "Why
don't you go down to the lobby ahead of
me?"

Michelle's eyes widened. "But Dad said
we have to stay together."

"He *also* said that I'm in charge," Stephanie reminded her. "And I say you can go
down to the lobby!"

Michelle grinned. "Really?" she asked.

"Sure. You're old enough to be alone for
a few minutes," Stephanie told her.

"Great!" Michelle exclaimed.

"But *only* go to the chocolate shop,"
Stephanie added. "There are lots of hotel
employees around there, so you won't
really be by yourself. Do you think you can
handle it?"

"Definitely," Michelle replied. She put the
business card her dad had given her and the
plastic card that was her room key in her belt
pack. Then she strapped it on. "I promise to

stay in the chocolate shop until you get there," she said solemnly.

"Great! So . . . what are you waiting for?" Stephanie grinned as Michelle raced to the door. "See you in a few minutes!" she called after her.

When Michelle was gone, Stephanie stared into her suitcase again. Michelle's problem was solved. But what about her own problem? What should she wear?

D.J.'s outfit was out of the question. Black bell-bottoms with brown flats? No way! Those fashion-crazy New Yorkers would think she was totally uncool.

She decided on her navy blue satin pants with the white racing stripes down the sides. She could pair them with her snug, long-sleeved navy T-shirt. That would look great with her new, thick-soled white sneakers. In fact, she'd seen a model wearing the exact same thing in the last issue of *Teen Style*.

I will look so great! she thought in excitement as she headed to the bathroom. *Correction,* she told herself, *I am going to use this chance to change myself into Sabrina. And she always looks fantastic! When I walk out of this hotel room, I will be an entirely different person—beautiful, self-confident, ultra-sophisticated. . . .*

Stephanie giggled as she looked at her messy reflection in the bathroom mirror. "Watch out, New York City!" she said aloud. "Sabrina Tanner is on her way!"

MICHELLE

Chapter 3

This is incredible," Michelle murmured. She stared at the rows and rows of chocolates in the glass display case.

"We do have some incredible candy," the saleslady agreed. "My name is Mrs. Dobbs. May I help you?"

Michelle giggled. Actually, she meant it was incredible that Stephanie actually let her go to the chocolate shop alone! It was hard being one of the youngest members of such a big household. Sometimes it seemed as if everyone except the twins bossed her around. It felt great to be on her own for once!

But Mrs. Dobbs was right. The store was amazing. Chocolate-covered almonds and caramels and mints filled the front of the glass case. Chocolate sculptures lined the shelves on the sides of the store. Michelle's eyes lingered over a milk chocolate cat and a snowman made of white chocolate.

Finally she pointed to some candies in the back row of the case. "I think I'll start with the chocolate-covered raisins," she said.

"Good choice!" Mrs. Dobbs handed Michelle a small gold bag filled with the treats. Michelle popped several into her mouth. "They're delicious, aren't they?" Mrs. Dobbs asked.

"Mmmm-Hmmm." Michelle nodded, because she knew it wasn't polite to talk with her mouth full.

She studied the other chocolates. "Wow! My oldest sister would love that little chocolate backpack," she said. "It looks just like her real one."

She pointed at the case again. "And I'll take two of those chocolate microphones, please. They're perfect for my uncle Jesse and our friend Joey," she added. "They have their own radio show in San Francisco."

"I see! So they talk into a *real* microphone all the time. That *is* perfect." Mrs. Dobbs tucked the backpack and two microphones into plastic containers. "Do you want anything else?" she asked.

"Yes. I *have* to buy those racing cars for my twin cousins, Nicky and Alex."

Mrs. Dobbs smiled. "It sounds like you have a very large family. Are they all back in San Francisco?"

"Yup, and all in the same house," Michelle told her. "You see, my mom died when I was really young. So my uncle Jesse and my dad's friend Joey moved into our house to help raise me and my two sisters. And then Jesse got married to Aunt Becky and they had the twins. So there's a lot of people I need to get souvenirs for. But now I've got them all!"

"I see," Mrs. Dobbs said. She totaled up Michelle's purchases. "That will be fourteen dollars and thirty-six cents, please."

Michelle's eyes widened. Things were really expensive in New York! She opened her belt pack. "Oh no!" she said. "I put everything in here *except* my money! I-I left it upstairs in my room."

"That's not a problem," Mrs. Dobbs told her. "Would you like to charge your purchases to your room?"

"Sure!" Michelle said. "So . . . could I have some more chocolate-covered raisins?"

A young girl hurried into the store. She smoothed back her dark brown hair as she stepped up to the candy counter.

"Six chocolate-covered pretzels, please," the girl ordered.

Michelle stared at her in amazement. "Kaye!" she exclaimed. "What are *you* doing *here?*"

Kaye Bloom went to Michelle's school back in San Francisco. She was one grade ahead of her, so Michelle didn't know her very well. But everyone knew who Kaye was— she wore the most stylish clothes and had all the latest toys. Kaye was one of the most popular girls in the school.

Kaye's mouth fell open when she recognized Michelle. "Michelle?" she said. "What are *you* doing here?"

Michelle laughed. "I'm on a vacation with my dad and my sister Stephanie," she replied.

Kaye smiled. "I'm on vacation with my family, too! Are you staying at this hotel?"

"Yup." Michelle nodded.

"That's so weird!" Kaye said. "I'm staying here, too!"

"It's not weird—it's great!" Michelle told her. "I can't believe I actually know somebody my age in New York City."

"You're not my age," Kaye reminded her. "I'm eleven."

"That's only a year older than me," Michelle said. *Is everyone going to treat me like a baby?* she wondered.

"I guess." Kaye looked around. "Where's your dad?"

"He's working now. So I came down here alone," Michelle explained. "But I'm waiting for my sister."

"I'm here on my own," Kaye said. "My parents let me go lots of places by myself. This trip is my birthday present. My parents said I can do whatever I want while we're in New York. So I picked spending the day at FAO Schwarz."

"What's FAO Schwarz?" Michelle asked. "Some kind of amusement park?"

Kaye rolled her eyes as if Michelle's questions were really dumb. "Of course not! I thought everybody knew about FAO Schwarz," she said. "I've known about it *forever*."

Michelle felt her cheeks flush in embarrassment.

"It's only the best toy store in the whole world," Kaye went on. "They have humongous stuffed animals, miniature cars that you can really drive, high-powered telescopes, the latest video games, and dolls from all over the world. And they just set up a special area for laser tag!"

"Wow," Michelle said. "That sounds incredible. I wish I could go."

"Have you ever played laser tag?" Kaye asked.

"No," Michelle admitted.

"It is *so* cool," Kaye told her. "When you hit someone with your laser beam, it makes a great noise. But if you get hit in the head, you're out of the game."

"Really?" Michelle asked. "Wow! That's awesome."

"I know. FAO Schwarz is the most incredible store." Kaye paused. "So, what are you doing the rest of the day?"

"Uh . . ." Michelle hesitated. She couldn't tell Kaye she was stuck in the hotel—doing nothing, while her big sister *baby-sat* her!

"I'm not sure yet," she finally answered.

"Too bad you can't come with me," Kaye said.

"I know. I mean, I *could* go," Michelle told her. "I just haven't made up my mind what I want to do yet."

Kaye frowned. "I thought your sister had to take care of you. Since you're just ten."

"I didn't say that," Michelle protested. "She doesn't have to take care of me. I just promised to hang out with her, so she wouldn't be bored," she added.

A tall, brown-haired woman burst into the store. "Kaye! What's taking so long? We're waiting!" she called.

Kaye's face turned bright red. *"Okay,*

Mom!" she said. "I'm just talking to a friend."

"A friend?" Mrs. Bloom smiled at Michelle. Kaye introduced them. "Are you here all alone?" Mrs. Bloom asked.

"Oh, no," Michelle answered. "My dad is working. And my big sister is up in our room."

"Really?" Mrs. Bloom looked surprised. "They let you wander around the hotel on your own? That doesn't sound right. Maybe you should come with us."

Michelle's heart leapt. "Go to FAO Schwarz? That would be fantastic," she said. "But . . . uh, I don't know if—"

"You don't know if your big sister will let you, do you?" Kaye asked.

Michelle straightened her shoulders. "I told you, I can do what I want."

"Well, then it's decided," Mrs. Bloom said. "You're coming with us, Michelle. Would you like me to call your father first?"

"Call my dad?" Michelle quickly thought about it. Her dad left Stephanie in charge. So, if Stephanie said she could go . . . then she could go!

Her eyes sparkled with excitement. "You

don't have to call my dad," she said. "I just have to tell my sister."

"Terrific!" Mrs. Bloom smiled. "Go do that. We'll meet you back in the lobby."

"Okay!" Michelle ran into the lobby and found an empty elevator. She rode to the fortieth floor and slipped her key card into the door to her room. She flung it open.

"Stephanie! I have a big favor to ask you!" she announced. The room was empty. She heard the shower running in the bathroom. Stephanie was *still* getting ready!

She knocked loudly on the bathroom door. "Steph!" she shouted.

"What?" Stephanie demanded. Her voice sounded muffled over the sound of the water.

"I met a friend from home," Michelle called. "She asked me to go to FAO Schwarz. Can I?"

"What?" Stephanie shouted back.

Michelle raised her voice. "Can I go out with Kaye Bloom to FAO Schwarz?"

"Do what?" Stephanie yelled.

Michelle groaned. "I said—can I go out with Kaye Bloom?"

Two on the Town

"Fine, Michelle!" Stephanie shouted back. *"Just don't go anywhere else!"*

Why would I want to go anywhere else? Michelle wondered.

"No problem!" she called to Stephanie. She clapped her hands together in excitement. *Excellent!* she thought. *Laser tag, here I come!*

"Thanks, Steph!" she yelled. "You're the best!"

"What?" Stephanie replied.

Michelle laughed. "Never mind!"

She put her twenty-dollar bill in her waist pack. Then she put on her green *Wake Up, San Francisco* jacket and headed out the door. This was turning into a great day after all!

Chapter
4

The game room?" Stephanie repeated. She turned up the hot water in the shower. Why couldn't Michelle just wait in the chocolate shop? Leave it to her to change their plans!

Well, it wasn't worth worrying about. Stephanie had seen the signs pointing to the game room down in the hotel lobby. She knew Michelle could spend hours playing dumb video games. So maybe it wasn't such a bad idea. After all, it would give her more time to get ready.

She picked up the wet, soapy shampoo bottle and read the instructions on the back for a third time.

"For super shiny hair, massage gently into scalp for four minutes."

Stephanie sighed and kept massaging her long, blond hair. She didn't have her watch in the shower. How was she supposed to know when four minutes were up?

Maybe if she counted to a thousand or something.

"One, two, three, four . . ." she began.

She lost count after two hundred and six. "Oh, forget it," Stephanie mumbled in frustration. She rinsed out the shampoo.

So much for Sabrina's super shiny hair! she thought as she reached for a towel. Then she spotted two fluffy white bathrobes hanging on the back of the door.

"Excellent!" She pulled on the hotel robe. She used the hotel hair dryer to style her hair. Then she swept her hair up in a French twist and pinned it. Finally she brushed out one long strand over her left eye.

She put on the navy outfit she'd chosen before.

Finished! She anxiously examined herself in the full-length mirror. Nope, she definitely needed to complete her outfit—something sophisticated to tie the look together. She put on her navy blue jacket.

Now she looked great! Stephanie smiled at her reflection. It was easy to imagine that she was really Sabrina Tanner, the ultimate New York model.

She tied the laces on her white sneakers. She grabbed her shoulder bag. Then she locked the room and hurried downstairs.

The lobby was crowded. A whole busload of people had just arrived and were waiting to check in. Stephanie scanned the crowd, just to see if anyone looked interesting. They were all adults—not one teen in the whole group!

Stephanie started toward the game room. She stopped as a boy around her age suddenly rushed through the revolving doors. He stood on tiptoe, scanning the crowd.

Now, he is a real New Yorker, Stephanie thought.

The boy wore a black turtleneck under a beat-up leather jacket, with jeans and running shoes. His light brown hair was long at the top and shaved close to his scalp underneath.

He looked totally cool. Stephanie was sure *he* was exactly the kind of guy a girl like Sabrina would go for.

He must have felt her watching him because he suddenly turned his head and stared right at her.

Stephanie felt her cheeks flush. She couldn't believe he caught her staring at him!

"Excuse me!" The boy rushed over to her. "Can you help me?" He started talking really fast.

"It's just that I was supposed to meet my dad here around eleven, and I'm a little late. I'm always late!" he went on. "Anyway, he's pretty tall, with light brown hair, like mine. But not cut like mine. And he's wearing a leather jacket, too."

"Oh. Well, uh . . . t-tall man, jacket . . . I don't know," Stephanie stuttered, feeling foolish. "I mean, it's pretty crowded in here."

The boy laughed. "Sorry," he said. "I guess it is. It's just that I saw you watching the crowd, so I thought—" He hesitated, then peered at Stephanie more closely.

She felt her heart speed up. He was *so* cute!

"Uh, let me start over," he said. "I'm Jordan Daniels. And I'm actually a pretty normal guy." He grinned, showing off an adorable dimple. His brown eyes twinkled with fun.

Stephanie grinned back. For a minute they stood there, smiling at each other.

"Um, why don't you check with the front desk," Stephanie finally suggested. "If your dad is running late, maybe he left a message for you."

"Good idea." Jordan nodded. "Hang on, I'll be right back."

Stephanie watched Jordan push through the crowd and make his way to the desk. He spoke to the clerk, then turned and hurried back toward Stephanie.

"He *did* leave a message!" Jordan told her. "Turns out he can't meet me at *all*. I would have waited here for nothing if it weren't for you. Thanks, uh . . . what's your name?"

"Ste—" Stephanie caught herself. "Sabrina," she said. "Sabrina Tanner." It sounded funny when she heard it out loud.

But, hey, what better way to really feel like Sabrina? She had the hairdo and the name. Now all she needed was the right attitude. To start with, she told herself, Sabrina wouldn't be shy around boys.

"Are you and your dad staying here, too?" Stephanie asked.

"No way." Jordan shook his head. "We live in Chelsea. That's down in the twenties," he explained. "But I help my dad at work sometimes. He got me out of school today so I could meet him here."

"Why here?" Stephanie asked.

"Oh. Because a lot of the stars my dad works with stay at this hotel," Jordan began to explain. "And their—"

"Stars?" Stephanie interrupted. "Like movie or TV stars?"

Jordan seemed a little embarrassed. "Yeah, well, he's sort of in show business," he said.

"Really? Wow! So is *my* dad!" Stephanie exclaimed.

Jordan's eyes widened. "Is your dad an actor?" Stephanie almost burst out laughing. "Hardly," she replied. "He produces and hosts a television show back in San Francisco. That's where I'm from," she added.

"Wow! That's sounds cool!" Jordan said.

"No cooler than working with big stars," Stephanie said. "I bet your dad knows some really famous people."

Jordan shrugged. "Well, I guess the most famous is Lee McMasters," he said.

"Lee McMasters?" Stephanie nearly shrieked in excitement. "I love his movies! He is the *best* action star ever! I can't *believe* you know him! I—"

Stephanie suddenly felt embarrassed. After all, she was supposed to be cool, hip Sabrina. And Sabrina wouldn't gush over some movie star like just any kid.

"So, why are you here?" Jordan asked.

Stephanie was glad he'd changed the subject.

"My dad had to tape a big interview with somebody who wouldn't leave New York," she explained. "He's busy working today. So, I'm just kind of hanging out."

"I guess I am, too." Jordan grinned at her again. "Hey, I'm kind of hungry," he said. "I skipped breakfast to get here. They have this fifties-style snack bar in the hotel. Want to come with me?"

Stephanie felt her heart start to beat with excitement. This incredibly cute and nice New Yorker had just invited *her* to lunch!

She forced herself to play it cool. "That sounds okay," she said.

"They have great onion rings," Jordan told her.

Stephanie loved onion rings, but all she said was "Really?"

Jordan led them to a booth in the back of the snack bar. They ordered a large plate of onion rings and two sodas. Then they studied the listings on the jukebox. Jordan insisted that she choose the first four songs.

The music blasted out and Stephanie leaned back. She was already having a great time.

"So, is this your first visit to New York?" Jordan asked.

Stephanie was about to say yes. Then she thought that someone like *Sabrina* probably came to New York lots of times.

"Oh, no," she told Jordan. "I've been here a few times."

"Did you stay at this hotel?" he asked.

"Uh, no, a different one," she replied.

"Which one?" he asked.

Stephanie gulped. "I . . . I can't remember the name. It's, um, uptown I think."

"On the West Side, or the East Side?" Jordan asked.

Stephanie felt her face grow hot. She had no idea where there *were* any hotels!

"Uh, the East Side," she said. "Do you miss a lot of school when you work with your father?" she asked, changing the subject.

"Sometimes I do," Jordan said. "But it's fun, even though I really have to work hard. Some of his stars are so demanding! Once, I had to chase all over town looking for this special kind of bottled water."

"Really? Who made you do that?" Stephanie asked.

Jordan looked uncomfortable. "I can't mention any names," he said. "You know how it is. Privacy and all that."

"Oh, of course," Stephanie said. She tried not to sound disappointed. After all, Sabrina would know exactly how it is.

"You must get a lot of those same questions," Jordan told her. "I mean, since your dad is famous and all."

"Famous?" Stephanie nearly choked on her cola. Her dad was fairly well known in the Bay Area. But he mostly interviewed local personalities. *Wake Up, San Francisco* wasn't exactly a high-glamour show.

"Well, I guess he *does* work with famous people," she said. "We've even had some of them over for dinner."

Of course, the last "famous" person her father brought home for dinner was a guy who invented a line of cleaning products that wouldn't harm the environment. Only Danny Tanner, who was a total neat freak, could have gotten so excited about this guy.

Stephanie tried to look bored by the whole subject. "My father's schedule is really crazy. He never knows when he'll have to go out of town for an interview. Or worse, when some celebrity is going to cancel on him."

"Tell me about it," Jordan said. He smiled at her. "Actually, a celebrity canceling is the reason you and I just met. It all happened because Lily O'Connor had a dentist appointment."

"Lily O'Connor?" Stephanie asked. "The talk show host?" Stephanie and her friends adored Lily O'Conner. They all watched her show nearly every day after school.

Jordan nodded. "Yeah, well, I was supposed to help my dad on a commercial with her today. But she canceled. She had to have a tooth pulled or something."

"I can't believe you were going to meet Lily O'Connor! That is so cool!" Stephanie exclaimed.

"Do *you* want to meet her?" Jordan asked. "Because I could probably get you tickets for tomorrow's show. If you're interested."

Stephanie's eyes widened. "Interested? Of course! I—"

Hold on, she told herself. *Sabrina wouldn't act so impressed. Chill!*

"Well, sure . . . that would be nice," she said. "If you can get the tickets. And if I'm not busy."

"I'm pretty sure I can get them," Jordan said. Stephanie wanted to leap up from the table. She wanted to race upstairs and call her friends and tell them all to watch for her on TV tomorrow!

Just wait until Michelle heard. She was a big Lily O'Connor fan, too.

Michelle! Stephanie gulped. Michelle was still in the game room.

"What's wrong?" Jordan asked.

"Oh, nothing much," Stephanie answered. But inside she was thinking, *Nothing much? I'm supposed to stay with Michelle. We're in a strange city, and Dad is depending on me to make sure she's safe and doesn't get lost.*

And I just forgot all about her!

Chapter
5

Michelle spotted Kaye as soon as she reached the lobby.

"All set!" Michelle exclaimed. "This is so exciting. Just wait until my friends Cassie and Mandy hear about FAO Schwarz. They are going to be so jealous!"

Kaye grabbed Michelle's arm and pulled her behind a huge potted palm. "Listen," Kaye said. "I'm letting my parents come with us, okay? It's just that they have some shopping to do. You know, to buy me more birthday gifts and stuff."

"Whatever," Michelle said. She didn't really care how many people came along. All

44

she cared about was getting out of the hotel—and going to the greatest toy store in the world!

"So, do they let you play laser tag as long as you want?" she asked Kaye. "Or is there a time limit?"

"I'm not sure," Kaye admitted. "But about my parents—it's not like we have to hang out with them or anything."

"Okay," Michelle said. She shrugged. She didn't really expect the Blooms to let her and Kaye go off in New York by themselves.

"All right, then." Kaye smiled. "Let's go."

Mrs. Bloom waved to them, and Kaye and Michelle hurried across the lobby.

Mrs. Bloom looked at Michelle. "Shouldn't we leave a message for someone, so they'll know where you're going?" she asked.

"I already told my sister where I'm going," Michelle said. "She said it was fine."

"I know, but I'd feel better if you left a note as well," Mrs. Bloom insisted. "You can tell her we'll be back by two o'clock."

"Okay," Michelle said. Parents were weird sometimes. If it made Mrs. Bloom feel better, she'd write a note.

She walked up to the hotel desk. "Can I leave I note for my sister?" she asked.

The clerk handed her a piece of paper, and she quickly wrote a message:

Went to FAO Schwarz. I promise to be back by two. Michelle

She folded the note and addressed it to Stephanie Tanner, Room 4014.

The clerk put the note in the slot for their room.

Mrs. Bloom studied Michelle as they turned to go. "Will you be warm enough in that jacket?" she asked.

Michelle glanced down at her green *Wake Up, San Francisco* windbreaker. She wasn't the least bit cold.

"I'm okay," she said.

Mrs. Bloom was really different from the way Kaye described her, Michelle thought. She sure didn't seem like the kind of parent who would let Kaye do anything she wanted. In fact, Mrs. Bloom sounded a lot like her own father—a big worrier!

Mrs. Bloom led Michelle and Kaye across

the lobby and through the revolving doors.
Mr. Bloom stood waiting on the sidewalk
outside.

"I need to make one stop before we go to
the toy store," he told Mrs. Bloom. "I'll drop
off a letter for a business associate. Then we
can go right back down to FAO Schwarz."

Mr. Bloom nodded to a doorman in a
fancy uniform. The doorman raised his arm
in the air as he blew a shiny silver whistle.
A yellow taxi screeched to a halt right in
front of him.

Mr. Bloom slid into the front seat, next to
the driver. Mrs. Bloom climbed into the back.
Kaye and Michelle sat next to her.

Mr. Bloom gave the driver the address of
his business associate as the cab pulled away
from the curb.

Mr. Bloom turned around in the front seat.
"I'm glad you're coming with us," he told
Michelle. "It's better than leaving you on
your own all day. Where is your father,
anyway?"

"He's working," Michelle explained.

"Well, you can stick close to us," Mrs.
Bloom said. "We'll take good care of you."

"Okay. Thanks." Michelle leaned back in her seat. She was enjoying her first New York cab ride.

"Look at that!" Kaye pointed out the window.

Michelle saw an old-fashioned horse-drawn carriage turn to go through the park. The driver wore a shiny black top hat. "It's like something from a movie," she said.

Around them, the cars and buses ground to a halt. Horns blared.

"This traffic is even worse than in the Bay Area!" Mrs. Bloom said.

"Mom!" Kaye said. She was almost bouncing with excitement. "It's a fashion shoot!"

"It is!" Michelle said breathlessly.

The traffic was stopped because a photographer was set up on the sidewalk, shooting two tall, stunning women. The models wore tight dresses; loose, flowing capes; and very high heels. They strutted across Fifth Avenue, stopping now and then to smile at the camera.

"They are totally glamorous," Michelle said.

"Awesome," Kaye added. "I've never seen anyone so beautiful."

"That'll do it!" the photographer shouted. "Thank you, everyone." He and his assistant began to pack up the camera equipment. The models ducked into a waiting limousine, and the traffic started moving again.

Stephanie would have really liked to see that, Michelle thought. She glanced out the back window. The Windsor was no longer in sight. Where was her sister now? she wondered.

For the first time, Michelle felt strange about going out with the Blooms. After all, her dad had told her *not* to leave the hotel. And to stick with her sister.

Stephanie said their father put *her* in charge. And Stephanie definitely said it was all right for her to go with Kaye.

So stop worrying! Michelle scolded herself. *You have the whole afternoon to do really cool New York stuff. You even have a friend to do it with!*

Michelle watched out the window as buses and cars rushed past their taxi. This was exactly what she wanted. She was in New York City, almost on her own, and about to go to the best store in the world.

This must be the coolest day of my life, Michelle decided. *Nothing can keep me from having major, major fun!*

Chapter
6

Michelle! Stephanie thought. She fought down a wave of fear. *What kind of sister am I? How could I forget all about her?*

She glanced at her watch. It was already after twelve-thirty! Michelle had been on her own for over an hour and a half. News stories about crime in New York started to flash through Stephanie's mind. Anything could have happened to her sister by now!

Okay, don't panic, she told herself. Michelle was safe in the game room. After all, there were probably dozens of games, and Michelle could spend *hours* just playing her favorite, Ski Slalom Challenge. Plus there

51

would be all sorts of hotel staff looking out for the kids there.

"Hey, Sabrina, is something wrong?" Jordan asked. "You look upset all of a sudden."

"Uh, no," Stephanie said quickly. "I'm not upset."

"Good," Jordan said. "Because I was thinking, maybe you and I could hang out for the rest of the day."

Stephanie drew in her breath. Wow! Hanging out with Jordan would be *amazing*. He was exactly the kind of guy she pictured Sabrina with.

This was her one chance to have a sophisticated New York date. She might even get to meet some of the celebrities Jordan knew.

But I can't run off and leave Michelle totally on her own, she realized.

She had to figure out what to do about her little sister.

For a second she wondered if she should tell Jordan about Michelle. *No*, she decided. *It was too uncool. Sabrina Tanner would never have to stay cooped up in a hotel, baby-sitting her bratty younger sister!*

Stephanie thought fast. She could run to the game room, find Michelle, and tell her to stay there for a couple of *more* hours. Then she could hang out with Jordan until four o'clock.

Sure—why not? It wasn't a brilliant plan. But at the moment it was the best she could come up with. All she had to do was get rid of Jordan for a few minutes so she could arrange things with Michelle.

"Hanging out would be great," she told Jordan. "But I really need to make a phone call first."

"No problem," Jordan said. "I should probably call about those tickets, too."

Stephanie reached for her shoulder bag and counted out enough money to pay her share of the check. "Let's each find a phone. I'll run to the ladies' room first, and then I'll meet you in the lobby. Say, in ten minutes?"

"Sure," Jordan agreed. "See you in ten."

Stephanie grinned. Things were working out perfectly!

She gathered her things together, then strolled into the ladies' room. She waited a few moments, then peeked out. She saw Jordan just leaving the snack shop.

She waited a few seconds more, then hurried into the hallway. She followed the signs to the game room, keeping an eye out for Jordan the whole time.

Screeech! Blaam! Whirrrr!

The sounds of dozens of video games all going at once grew louder as she approached the double doors marked GAME ROOM.

She swung the doors open, covered her ears with both hands, and scanned the room for Michelle.

Ski Slalom Challenge! The bright blue and white machine stood in the middle of the center aisle. Stephanie headed right toward it.

But Michelle wasn't there. Two boys were fighting over the game.

Stephanie turned, looking from machine to machine. There was no sign of Michelle anywhere.

That's strange, Stephanie thought. *Michelle said she was going to the game room.*

She felt a pang of worry. It *had* been an awfully long time since Michelle went downstairs. *But she wouldn't change our plans, I know it,* Stephanie thought.

Okay, stay calm, she told herself. But how was she supposed to stay calm when her sister had vanished?

I'll do a thorough search, Stephanie decided. She would walk around the edge of the room, then go down each of the aisles be tween the machines.

Please, Michelle, be here! she said to herself.

Stephanie walked around and through the aisles—three times. She checked every game in the room. Still no sign of her sister.

She must have gone to the bathroom, Stephanie thought. It was the only thing that made sense.

She spotted a clerk in a red jacket with the Windsor hotel insignia on his pocket. He seemed to be in charge of the game room. She hurried over to him and tapped him on the arm.

"Excuse me," Stephanie began. "But did you happen to see a ten-year-old girl with blond hair? She's wearing a white sweatshirt over black leggings."

The clerk shook his head. "Sorry," he said.

"But there's no way I can keep track of all the kids who come in here."

Stephanie's heart fluttered. "But she's my little sister! I'm in charge of her. Are you sure you didn't see her? She probably played Ski Slalom Challenge for about an hour and a half."

"Hey, mister," a kid interrupted them. "Motorcycle Mayhem is stuck. The lights just keep blinking."

"Sorry." The clerk turned away from Stephanie and went to find out what the problem was with the game.

"Thanks for all your help," Stephanie mumbled.

Okay, she told herself. *There's nothing to worry about. Michelle probably ran out of quarters. Sure, that's it! She probably went back to our room to find more change.*

Stephanie flew into the lobby and grabbed the first empty elevator up to her floor. She put the plastic card in the lock, opened the door, and raced inside the room.

She scanned the room, looking for Michelle. Not on the beds. The bathroom door was open, the bathroom empty.

The phone began ringing.

Michelle!

Stephanie grabbed up the receiver. "Michelle, where are you?" she demanded.

"It's not Michelle, it's me—Allie!" a voice answered.

"Allie?" Stephanie said in surprise. "Why are you calling?"

"Because we thought it would be fun," Darcy chimed in. Both of Stephanie's best friends giggled.

"We were right by the school pay phone where we usually meet," Allie explained. "We miss you!"

"So I used my phone card to call you," Darcy added. "We can talk for only one second. Are you having fun yet?"

"I met a totally gorgeous guy—Jordan," Stephanie said. "His father is a famous director and he promised me tickets to the taping of *The Lily O'Connor Show* tomorrow!"

Darcy and Allie squealed so loudly, Stephanie had to pull the phone away from her ear.

"That's amazing!" Darcy exclaimed.

"Yeah, but right now Michelle is missing," Stephanie added. "I'm supposed to hang out with Jordan, but I can't do anything until I find her."

"You must be furious," Allie said.

"More like worried out of my mind," Stephanie replied.

"Michelle's a smart kid. I'm sure she's okay," Darcy said.

"Probably," Stephanie agreed, "but I'll feel a lot better when I find her. Listen, tell everyone at school to watch the show tomorrow. And look for me in the audience, okay? I'll tell you more later. Oh, and tape the show for me, okay?"

"Definitely!" Darcy promised.

Stephanie hung up the phone. She double-checked to make sure Michelle wasn't in the bathroom or in their father's room. But there was no sign of her.

With a sigh, Stephanie headed back down to the lobby.

This is nuts! she thought. *Now everyone is going to watch for me on* The Lily O'Connor Show. *And if I don't get back to Jordan, I won't even be on it. Michelle is spoiling everything for me!*

There was no way she could check every shop in the hotel to ask about Michelle. Jordan would be waiting in the lobby. . . .

That's it! She could ask the doorman in the lobby. *Maybe he saw Michelle!*

Stephanie raced into the lobby. Luckily, there was no sign of Jordan yet. *Getting the tickets must be taking him a while,* Stephanie thought gratefully. She ran over to the doorman.

"Excuse me," she began. "I'm trying to find my little sister. She's ten and about so tall. She's got long, blond hair, and she's wearing a white sweatshirt with black pants."

The doorman frowned. "I think I *did* see her," he said. "But she was wearing a green jacket that said, *Wake Up, San Francisco* on the back."

"That's her!" Stephanie said excitedly. "It's got to be!" No one else in New York would have a jacket from their dad's show.

The doorman smiled. "Well, she left the hotel about twenty minutes ago."

"She *what?*" Stephanie couldn't believe she heard him correctly. "She couldn't have!"

"She did," the doorman said. "Is that a problem?"

"A problem?" Stephanie repeated. She groaned and put her hand to her forehead. "Only the biggest problem of my life!"

Chapter
7

"Oh, wow!" Michelle exclaimed excitedly. She followed Kaye through the door of the toy store. "Look at this place. I can't believe these stuffed animals!"

The front of the store was lined with gigantic furry creatures. Michelle shook the paw of an enormous brown bear. "He's almost as tall as my dad!" she said.

Kaye laughed. "I bet that pink *Brontosaurus* is taller."

Michelle gaped at the huge toy. Its head almost brushed the ceiling.

"Check that out!" Kaye said. She pointed to a round silver spaceship. It was making a humming sound and hovering just above a red launching pad.

Michelle felt her jaw drop. "It looks like it's going to take off any second now!"

A salesman pressed a remote control. The spaceship zoomed toward Michelle and Kaye, circled them, then returned to its launching pad.

"This is so great!" Michelle said happily. *A totally fabulous store*, she thought. *And no one looking over my shoulder! No one telling me what to do. Coming here with Kaye was the best idea ever!*

"It is pretty awesome," Kaye agreed. "Let's go upstairs." She pointed to a store directory. "That's where the laser tag is."

Michelle followed Kaye to a long escalator.

"Girls. Wait for us, please!" Mr. Bloom called as he hurried after them. "You're getting too far ahead!"

"Kaye," Mrs. Bloom added. "Don't go running off."

"Wait! Your mom and dad—" Michelle began as she stepped on the escalator. "They just said—"

Two on the Town

"Don't worry. They'll catch up," Kaye told Michelle.

Michelle glanced behind her. Mrs. Bloom was at the bottom of the escalator, calling up to them. Michelle couldn't make out what she was saying.

"Kaye, wait," Michelle tried again. "Your mom really wants to tell you something." She knew that if she ever ignored her father that way, she'd be in major trouble.

"My mom probably just wants to make sure I have enough money," Kaye said. "I told you, I'm allowed to be on my own. Besides, I have a set plan with my parents. We always split up, then meet at the store entrance. So let's go play laser tag. We'll meet my parents later."

"Okay," Michelle replied. She thought it was great that the Blooms were so trusting. Maybe she could get them to talk to her father.

The two girls stepped off the escalator and followed a purple neon sign that said LASER TAG—THIS WAY!

Flashing lights flickered across the ceiling.

Dance music was playing, and kids were shouting with excitement.

A young woman greeted them. "Hi, I'm Tina," she said. "Welcome to laser tag! It's our newest toy. Kids can try it out and play for five minutes in the laser room. Are you interested?"

"You bet!" Michelle exclaimed. Tina told her and Kaye to take off their shoes and put them in a cubbyhole.

"You guys are so lucky," Tina went on. "You came at just the right time. There isn't even a line!"

Michelle and Kaye tucked their shoes into a cubbyhole. Tina handed them their laser equipment. They each had a vest, a headband, and a laser blaster.

"The vest has a sensor box sewn into it," Tina explained. "When someone zaps you, it flashes and makes a noise." She aimed her blaster at Michelle's vest and pushed a red button.

The sensor light flashed and a noise like a siren wailed.

"The headband has a sensor, too," Tina said. "It flashes if you get hit in the head, and then you're out of the game. So try to duck."

Tina handed Michelle and Kaye their blasters.

"Remember, all you have to do is aim and push the red button. Have fun!" Tina told them.

Michelle and Kaye stepped inside the darkened laser room. Bright red, green, and yellow lights made the room feel like the inside of a big spaceship. Michelle blinked until her eyes adjusted to the dark.

Kaye gasped. "This is incredible!"

"Look at my sweatshirt!" Michelle told Kaye. The lights lit up her clothes, making her white sweatshirt glow purple.

"Cool!" Kaye pulled her trigger and blasted Michelle. Michelle's vest sensor rang out.

"Got you!" Kaye cried.

"Hey!" Michelle exclaimed. "I didn't know we were ready to start."

"Too bad," Kaye told her. "You'd better run. Or else you'll be toast!" She aimed at Michelle again.

Michelle quickly lifted her own blaster and aimed at Kaye.

Ziiiing! Kaye's sensor went off.

"Okay, we're even," Kaye said. "Now, let's both push the button at the same time. One . . . two . . . three . . . go!"

Both girls pushed the red buttons and fell to the floor at the same moment. Their laser beams bounced off the walls. Michelle started to laugh. Kaye zapped her. Then Michelle zapped Kaye back.

"Let's see if we can make our laser beams cross on the wall!" Kaye said.

A buzzer sounded. An overhead light came on in the room, and the laser beams vanished.

"Time's up, girls!" Tina called. "Or do you want another session?"

"Let's do it again," Kaye said. "Let's play until they say we have to stop."

Michelle hesitated. "Isn't it getting close to lunchtime?" she asked. "Maybe we should look for your parents."

"Come on," Kaye said. "We have all day to eat lunch. Please, Michelle! I mean, how often do you get a chance to play laser tag in FAO Schwarz?"

Michelle grinned. "You're right," she told her. "After all, we can eat lunch any day. But playing laser tag here is a once-in-a-lifetime chance. And that's the kind of excitement I like!"

Chapter
8

Stephanie stared at the hotel doorman in disbelief. "No! My sister couldn't have left the hotel! Not in a taxi. And not with a family. *I'm* her family! There must be some mistake."

"I don't think so. I remember her jacket," the doorman said.

"But . . . but how could she have left without telling me?"

"Maybe she left you a message," the doorman suggested. "Why don't you check at the front desk?"

Stephanie's heart was pounding as she raced to the desk.

What was going on? It wasn't like Michelle to leave—not without asking. And it was definitely not like her to go anywhere *with strangers!*

Stephanie asked the desk clerk to check her room mailbox.

She couldn't believe it when the clerk pulled out a piece of paper. "Here's a message for Stephanie Tanner," the clerk said.

Stephanie grabbed the paper with shaking hands. She quickly read Michelle's message.

"I can't believe this!" Stephanie muttered. Michelle *had* left the hotel. She went to FAO Schwarz, whatever that was.

Stephanie moaned. Michelle had done some pretty dumb things before . . . but this had to be the dumbest! And it made no sense at all.

Michelle was responsible enough to tell me before she went to the game room, Stephanie thought. *Why would she leave the hotel without checking with me first?*

Because I was late, Stephanie realized. *I never showed up in the game room.*

She felt a terrible pang of guilt. It was all

her fault. Michelle waited and waited and finally left.

But it still makes no sense, Stephanie told herself.

Maybe she shouldn't have kept Michelle waiting so long. But that didn't mean Michelle could go running off with strangers!

Now Stephanie's day was ruined. She couldn't possibly go anywhere with Jordan. She had to find Michelle before her dad came back to the hotel and found out that Michelle was missing!

What rotten luck! Stephanie thought. She met a totally cool boy. A boy who could hang out with celebrities—but wanted to spend time with her instead! Now she *couldn't* spend time with him. All because her little sister was totally, completely irresponsible!

"Sabrina!" Jordan's voice rang out, interrupting Stephanie's thoughts. She jumped about a foot in the air.

"Uh, Jordan! H-hi," she stuttered.

"What's wrong?" Jordan asked.

"Nothing!" she replied.

"Are you sure?" He peered closer at her.

"What happened to you? Did you forget we were supposed to meet?"

"Of course not," she told him. "But, um, actually, I'm not sure we can hang out after all."

"We can't?" Jordan asked.

"Not unless we go to FAO Schwarz," Stephanie murmured.

"FAO Schwarz?" Jordan repeated. "Sure. That could be cool."

"It could?" Stephanie asked. "I mean, uh, of course it could!"

"Have you been there before?" Jordan asked.

"Oh, yeah. Sure, dozens of times," Stephanie replied.

"So, what are we waiting for?" Jordan grinned. "Let's go!"

Stephanie buttoned her jacket as she followed Jordan through the revolving doors.

"It's great that it's so close, we can walk there in a couple of minutes," Jordan said.

"Isn't it?" Stephanie replied. "But, um, I'll let you lead the way."

It's great that Jordan knows where to find FAO Schwarz. Because I have no idea what it is!

Stephanie thought. *But at least I can look for Michelle once we get there. I'll just make up some excuse to get away from Jordan and search for her.*

Stephanie gazed up at the impressive hotels that lined Fifth Avenue. "This looks like a nice neighborhood to live in," she said.

Jordan laughed. "Nice? You've got to be a millionaire to live here!"

"That's what I meant," she said.

Jordan stopped walking. "Here we are," he said.

Stephanie's jaw dropped in surprise. A toy store! A very *big* toy store!

"Uh, it looks . . . um, the same as always," she said.

"Well, yeah," Jordan said. He pulled her inside and past the gigantic stuffed animals without even glancing at them. "Let's see what the special displays are," he said.

Stephanie found herself staring at a huge display of beanbag animals. She and Michelle had collected almost seventy of them.

The one they wanted most was the panda. She and Michelle had been searching for one for weeks. All the stores at home were out of them.

Now, right in front of her, was a whole *stack* of pandas! She lifted one from the top of the stack.

Jordan came up behind her. "What is that?" he asked.

Uh-oh! Stephanie gulped. *Sabrina would collect CDs, designer clothes, exotic perfumes—but never stuffed toys!*

"Uh, it's this silly toy my little sister collects," she said.

"You have a little sister?" Jordan asked. "So do I!" He rolled his eyes. "I swear, sometimes she drives me straight up the wall. Believe me, no one else can possibly be such a total pain!"

"If you only knew," Stephanie murmured.

"So, are you buying it for her?" Jordan asked.

"Sure!" Stephanie said. "Um, though, I forget where the best cash registers are."

"Let's try upstairs," Jordan told her. "The lines are usually shorter up there."

"Okay," Stephanie said. They rode the escalator to the second floor. Stephanie scanned the store, hoping to catch a glimpse of Michelle.

Stephanie spotted a flashing purple neon sign: LASER TAG—THIS WAY! *That was exactly the kind of thing Michelle would love,* Stephanie thought. Maybe she was playing laser tag at this very minute.

"You know, it's too bad my sister Michelle isn't here," Stephanie said. "She would really love to try laser tag. I almost wish I could play it for her—so I could tell her about it," she added.

"Why not?" Jordan shrugged. "It's for little kids, but I'm willing to try."

"Okay," Stephanie said. "We don't have to stay long."

She and Jordan paid their fee, exchanged their shoes for laser equipment, and hurried into the laser room.

"Oh, wow!" Jordan laughed. "Check out your pants!" The bright lights made the white stripes on Stephanie's pants turn green and purple.

This could be fun, Stephanie thought. *If only I weren't so worried about finding Michelle!*

Ziiing!

74

Stephanie gasped in surprise as Jordan zapped her.

"Hey! At least give me a chance to turn my blaster on!" she exclaimed.

Jordan laughed and zapped her again. Stephanie hid behind a pillar and zapped him back. Jordan fell to the floor, pretending to be a dying alien.

Stephanie giggled. Jordan was so much fun! She couldn't believe he didn't mind playing laser tag!

"Kaye!"

Stephanie looked up as a woman hurried into the laser room. "Kaye? Are you in here?" The woman noticed Stephanie watching her. "Excuse me, but have you seen my daughter, Kaye?" she asked. "She's eleven, with light brown hair. I can't find her anywhere!"

"Sorry, I haven't seen her," Stephanie told her. *And I haven't seen Michelle, either,* she thought. Suddenly she realized how completely irresponsible she was being. She ought to be searching for her sister—not playing laser tag!

"This is terrible!" the woman exclaimed.

"I've been searching for Kaye for at least half an hour."

"If I see her, I'll tell her you're looking for her," Stephanie promised.

"Thank you," the woman said. She hurried away.

Jordan came up to Stephanie. "What was that about?"

"She was looking for her daughter," Stephanie explained. *Maybe I should just tell Jordan what's going on,* she thought. But what would he think of her when she explained that her little sister was lost in New York City and she was playing laser tag?

"That woman should just page her," Jordan commented. "That's the only way to find someone in a big store like this."

"You're right. I should have thought of that!" Stephanie exclaimed.

"It's okay," Jordan told her. "It's not your problem."

"Uh, right." Stephanie swallowed hard. *But it is my problem,* she thought. *And I should page Michelle right now!*

It might be the only way to find her sister.

But how could she page her without letting Jordan know what she was doing?

She thought quickly for a minute. "Um, listen, Jordan," she said. "I'm really thirsty. Would you wait here while I find a water fountain?"

"I'll come with you," Jordan offered.

"No!" Stephanie nearly shouted. "Uh, I'm going to come right back. Really. Just wait for me here."

Stephanie raced out of the laser room. The customer service desk was at the very back of the floor. She dashed past an antigravity chamber, a complete kid's kitchen, and displays of computers, board games, and miniature automobiles.

"My sister is missing," she gasped to the woman behind the customer service desk. "Can you page her?"

"Sure. What's her name?" the woman asked.

"Michelle Tanner." Stephanie gulped down a few deep breaths as the woman spoke into a microphone.

"Will Michelle Tanner please come to the customer service desk on the second floor?

Michelle Tanner," the woman repeated. She clicked off the microphone and turned to Stephanie. "It may take a while for her to answer."

"That's okay. I'll wait," Stephanie said. She paced up and down in front of the service desk. Her mind raced.

What if Michelle *wasn't* in the store? What if she wasn't back at the hotel by four o'clock? What would she tell her father?

Wait a minute! Stephanie thought. What if her dad called the hotel to talk to them—and they weren't there?

"I'll be right back," Stephanie told the clerk. She hurried to the pay phone hanging on a nearby wall. She pulled out the hotel's card, dialed the Windsor, and asked for the front desk.

"Hello? This is Stephanie Tanner," she told the desk clerk. "Do you know if my father, Danny Tanner, called our room?"

The clerk hesitated a minute. "Let me check, Miss Tanner." A moment later he said, "No, there are no messages."

"Okay, No, wait! I want to *leave* a message," she declared. "For Danny Tanner. If he calls our room, tell him that my sister and I are in the game room. We'll be there all afternoon, so he won't be able to reach us. But we'll definitely meet him back in our room at four o'clock."

The clerk read the message back and Stephanie hung up.

What a relief I thought of that! she realized. Now her dad *could* call in, but he'd get her message and think they were together. So he wouldn't worry.

Now all she could do was pray that Michelle was in the store and that she heard the paging announcement. And that she would come to the customer service desk—in about two seconds. Because Jordan was going to start wondering where she was, and—

"Stephanie!" a familiar voice called out behind her. "What are you doing here?"

Stephanie spun around. *"Michelle!"* she screamed. *"Where have you been?"*

Chapter
9

Where have *I* been?" Michelle stared at Stephanie. The last thing she expected to find in the toy store was her sister. "I've been right here. I told you," she said. "But what are *you* doing here?"

"What do you mean, what am *I* doing here?" Stephanie demanded. "I'm looking for you! You weren't supposed to leave the hotel, remember?"

"You said I could," Michelle replied.

Stephanie put her hands on her hips. "What are you talking about?" she asked. "I never said you could leave the hotel. You were supposed to wait in the chocolate shop.

All I ever said was that it was okay for you to go the game room."

"Game room?" Michelle tried to remember talking about a game room and couldn't. "What game room?"

"The one off the hotel lobby," Stephanie said. "You asked if I could meet you in the game room, instead."

"No, I didn't," Michelle insisted. "I asked if I could go out with the Blooms."

Stephanie seemed confused. "The Blooms? Who are the Blooms?"

"Mr. and Mrs. Bloom, and their daughter, Kaye," Michelle explained. "I know her from school. She's only the most popular girl in the fifth grade." She folded her arms across her chest. "What is wrong with you, anyway?" she asked. "You told me I could go when you were in the shower."

"No, I didn't," Stephanie insisted. "When I was in the shower, you said you were going to the *game room!*"

"I never said game room. I said Kaye Bloom." Michelle's blue eyes widened. *"Game room—Kaye Bloom.* Oh, no!" She burst out laughing.

"What's so funny?" Stephanie stared at her as if she were crazy.

"Don't you get it?" Michelle gasped with laughter. "I said Kaye Bloom—but you heard *game room!*"

Suddenly Stephanie burst out laughing, too. "I can't believe it! What a dumb misunderstanding!" Stephanie laughed so hard that tears ran from her eyes.

"You must have been really upset when you couldn't find me in the game room," Michelle finally said.

"Totally! I was furious," Stephanie replied. "But everything's fine now. So, where are the Blooms, anyway?"

"Well, Kaye and I were playing laser tag when I heard you page me," Michelle said. "So I came here. Kaye went to the doll department. She's waiting for me there."

"Kaye!" Stephanie exclaimed. "That's the girl who was lost."

"Kaye isn't lost," Michelle told her.

"But I saw her mother in the laser arena," Stephanie said. "She was frantic. She was looking everywhere for Kaye!"

"I don't know why," Michelle told her.

"Her parents agreed to meet us back at the front door."

"Well, you guys had better find her parents, and fast," Stephanie said. "They need to know you're okay. And I'd better find Jordan," she added.

"Jordan?" Michelle asked. "Who's Jordan?"

Stephanie smiled. "Jordan Daniels. I met him in the hotel lobby. He is so great! And guess what? He's going to get tickets for *The Lily O'Connor Show* tomorrow!"

Michelle's mouth dropped open. "How?" she asked.

"His father is a famous director," Stephanie replied. "He knows her personally or something. He can probably get us a whole bunch of tickets."

"Wow! Can I go, too?" Michelle asked.

"Maybe. If Dad lets you," Stephanie told her. "And if we—"

"Sabrina! Michelle!"

Sabrina? Michelle blinked in surprise as a cute guy rushed toward them.

"Who are you?" Michelle demanded. "And who's Sabrina?"

"Shhhh!" Stephanie kicked her in the ankle.

"Hey!" Michelle protested. She rubbed her ankle. Stephanie sure was acting weird.

"Uh, Michelle, this is Jordan," Stephanie said quickly. "Jordan, this is my sister, Michelle."

"I guessed that," Jordan said. He turned to Stephanie. "I heard the store page Michelle Tanner. And I remembered that was your last name." He frowned in confusion. "But I don't get it. How did you know Michelle was here?"

"Uh, I guessed," Stephanie blurted out.

"She's just kidding," Michelle said. "I told her I was coming here. I left her a note back at the hotel. Because *I* know how to be *responsible*," she added.

Stephanie flushed. "That's right, you were responsible, Michelle."

Michelle beamed. "Well, I *am* old enough to take care of myself," she said. She turned to Jordan. "I'm here with a friend of mine."

Stephanie thinks she's so cool and mature, she thought. *Well, I can be cool and mature, too!*

"Friend, huh?" Jordan said. "Well, I have

a great idea," he went on. "Why don't we all go eat lunch at Planet Hollywood?" He turned to Stephanie. "Unless you've been there a million times already."

"Well, not *too* many times," Stephanie began.

"You're inviting *all* of us?" Michelle interrupted. "Great! Let me get Kaye and—"

"Oh, Michelle!" Stephanie glared at her. "I think we need to go to the ladies' room for a second. Don't we?" She grabbed Michelle's sleeve and pulled her away.

"Uh, back in a minute, Jordan," Michelle called over her shoulder.

"Michelle, you don't understand," Stephanie began the instant they were inside the room.

"Wait! You don't have to explain anything," Michelle told her. "I know you want to fool Jordan some more."

"I'm not trying to fool him, okay?" Stephanie said.

"Oh, no? Then why does he think your name is Sabrina?" Michelle asked.

Stephanie's face reddened. "Okay, I suppose I wanted to fool him a *little*."

"Right," Michelle said.

"Please, Michelle," Stephanie went on. "I don't want to spend the rest of the day with you and the Blooms. I want to have lunch with Jordan alone."

"But it would be fun to go to Planet Hollywood," Michelle said. "I've never been there!"

Stephanie thought quickly. "Wouldn't it be more fun to stay here with Kaye, and do whatever *you* want to do?"

"Well, maybe," Michelle said.

"Great. As long as you stay with the Blooms," Stephanie told her. "And if you promise to go *right* back to the hotel afterward."

"I will, I will," Michelle said.

"Well, okay, then," Stephanie told her. "But remember, Dad will be back at four. So don't change the plans again," she added.

"Why would I want to?" Michelle asked. "FAO Schwarz is the best place I've ever been. I don't want to leave."

"Okay, then, it's a deal," Stephanie said. "Let's tell Jordan."

Michelle marched outside. Jordan was still

waiting in the hall. He smiled when he saw them. She had to admit—he *was* pretty cute. She could see why her sister wanted to impress him.

"Listen, you two go to lunch," Michelle told him. "I'd rather stay here with my friend Kaye."

Jordan shrugged. "Sounds good to me. Come on, Sabrina!"

Stephanie turned to Michelle. "Remember—meet me back at the hotel at four!"

"All right, *Sabrina!*" Michelle called back. Sometimes her sister was extrememly weird.

She watched as Stephanie and Jordan stepped onto the escalator. *Thank goodness they left!* Michelle thought. She couldn't wait to check out the doll department.

She was about to follow Stephanie and Jordan down the stairs, when she suddenly stopped short.

Dad! she groaned. Stephanie hadn't even thought about him! What if he called the hotel and they were *both* gone?

We should definitely leave a message for Dad, Michelle decided. *I can't believe Stephanie didn't think of it!*

87

Michelle dug a quarter from her pocket. She also pulled out the card with the hotel phone number on it.

She hurried to the pay phone, dialed, and asked for the front desk.

"Hi. I'd like to leave a message for my father, Danny Tanner, if he calls in," she told the clerk. "Please tell him that Michelle and Stephanie are with the Blooms for the day. We'll be eating lunch in the dining room. A really, really, long lunch!" she added.

Michelle smiled as she hung up the phone.

That will show Stephanie who the responsible one is! Now . . . back to my afternoon of fun!

Chapter 10

Wait until Darcy and Allie hear I ate lunch two feet away from Arnold Schwarzeneggar's motorcycle—the actual motorcycle he rode in the first Terminator *movie!*

Stephanie gazed happily around Planet Hollywood. It was the most amazing restaurant she'd ever seen.

The walls were covered with movie posters and clothes and props all the famous stars had used. She and Jordan were only one table away from the jacket Billy Baldwin wore in the movie *Backdraft*. And four tables away from Bruce Willis's senior high school yearbook!

"I guess all this stuff doesn't mean much to you," Jordan commented.

"Oh, of course it does," Stephanie protested. Then she remembered that she was supposed to be Sabrina, who had been here before. "I mean, it's *always* fun to see things from my favorite movies. No matter how many times I've already seen them."

"Yeah, I guess I feel the same way," Jordan told her.

"Really?" Stephanie leaned closer across the table. "So which famous stars have you met?" She hoped she sounded casual and matter-of-fact—as if she met famous stars every day.

Jordan seemed embarrassed. "Oh, I don't want to bore you," he said.

"Would you like an appetizer?" A waitress suddenly appeared at their table.

"Um, sure," Jordan said. "I'll have the chicken burritos."

Stephanie glanced at the menu and then again at the walls. Maybe she should order something that sounded very West Coast. After all, L.A. was every bit as hip as New

York. "I'll have the Surfer's Special," she told the waitress.

She smiled at Jordan. "I always order that whenever I'm in L.A."

The waitress took their drink orders and hurried off.

Jordan brushed back a shock of dark hair. He really was exceptionally cute. "Do you go to L.A. often?" he asked.

"My father flies there a lot," Stephanie lied. "You know, business." She remembered a TV show she'd seen on Hollywood. "The traffic is the worst, but I love the clubs."

Jordan's eyes widened. "They let you into the clubs there? Here in New York, you practically have to show your birth certificate to get in the door." He gave a rueful laugh. "My friends and I tried to get into a club once. It was a total disaster. The manager wound up calling my dad!"

Stephanie wanted to laugh with him. It was exactly the sort of disaster that would happen to her. But she knew that Sabrina would *not* identify with it. "They let me into the L.A. clubs *because* of my dad," she explained. "Everyone there knows him, and he's cool about it."

"You're lucky," Jordan said. "Not to mention brave."

"What do you mean?" Stephanie asked.

Jordan grinned at her. "You ordered the Surfer's Special—a whole plate full of raw oysters!"

Raw oysters? Stephanie thought. She hadn't read the menu very carefully. She just assumed the Surfer's Special would be things like fried shrimp or crab cakes. But raw oysters? She had never eaten a raw oyster in her life.

"I can't even imagine eating them," Jordan confessed. "They're so . . . slimy. It would be like swallowing eyeballs or something."

The image made Stephanie's stomach spin. Now there was *definitely* no way she could eat them.

"Um, you know, Jordan," she said. "It might be fun to get the same thing as you. I mean, I've had raw oysters a zillion times, and it's getting to be kind of a bore. Do you think it's too late to change my order to burritos?"

"I don't know," Jordan said. "Let's ask the waitress when she comes back with our drinks."

"Okay. I hope it isn't a problem," Stephanie said.

Jordan frowned. "Speaking of problems, I'm kind of having trouble getting those tickets."

"The tickets?" Stephanie repeated.

"To *The Lily O'Connor Show*," Jordan said. "You didn't forget, did you?"

"Oh, no! Of course not," Stephanie said.

Jordan looked upset. "It's just that my dad wasn't around when I called him before. And no one who works on the show knows *me* personally. So I'll have to get my dad to ask for the tickets."

"You mean you might *not* get them?" Stephanie asked.

"Well, the extra tickets might already be taken," he explained.

"But—I already told everyone back home to watch the show tomorrow," Stephanie said. "I told them I'd be in the audience."

"I'm sorry," Jordan said. "I really hope I *can* get them. But I—"

Eeeeeee!

A loud, shrill shriek rang out at the next table. Stephanie spun around and stared at the redheaded girl who screamed. The girl jumped up and pointed. Her face flushed a bright red.

"What is it? What's going on?" Stephanie asked.

"It-it's Lee McMasters!" the girl managed to say.

Stephanie gasped. *Lee McMasters!* She stared across the restaurant.

And nearly leapt out of her chair. The totally gorgeous Lee McMasters was crossing the room, heading right toward them.

"I can't believe this!" Stephanie could barely speak. One of her most favorite actors *ever* was about to walk past their table. This was her one and only chance to meet him.

She took a deep breath and turned to Jordan. "So, what are you waiting for?" she asked. "Don't you want to say hello?"

"Say hello?" Jordan looked at her blankly.

"To Lee McMasters," Stephanie said.

"Your dad knows him, remember? You told me they worked together."

"Oh. Right!" Jordan shifted in his seat.

"So, couldn't you say hi?" Stephanie urged. She was dying to ask Jordan if he would get Lee McMasters's autograph for her. But Sabrina would be far too cool for that. "Why don't you invite him over to our table?" she asked instead. "It'd be great to meet him."

Jordan nervously ran his fingers through his hair. "No, it's . . . I don't think that's such a good idea."

"Why not?" Stephanie asked.

"Well . . . because, I . . . because Lee hates invitations like that," Jordan answered. "He's a very private person."

"But he knows your dad," Stephanie said.

"Well, doesn't he know *your* dad, too?" Jordan shot back.

"My dad?" Stephanie echoed.

"Sure, Sabrina," Jordan said. "I thought your dad knew tons of famous actors."

Ulp! Stephanie felt herself blushing again. *I almost forgot I was Sabrina!*

She shrank back in her chair. "Uh, well,

um, he—" She suddenly wished she'd never thought of being Sabrina. She was getting awfully tired of having to pretend to be someone else.

"So, who have *you* met?" Jordan asked. He sounded seriously interested.

Stephanie winced. "Oh, I'm so bad at remembering names," she stalled. "Let's see. Hmmm. Who have I met? Do you mean recently?"

The waitress arrived and began to set their food on the table just as Lee McMasters walked past.

Saved, Stephanie thought. *Thank goodness!* The waitress was in the way—at least she didn't have to pretend Sabrina knew Lee McMasters.

She lowered her eyes—and stared at the plate that the waitress had set down in front of her. Little grayish-black ovals. Raw oysters. They definitely looked slimy. Stephanie had a horrible feeling that if she tried to swallow one, it would feel exactly like she was swallowing an eyeball!

Yuck! she thought. *And double yuck!* Her

stomach churned. She was afraid she might pass out.

"I guess it's too late to change your order," Jordan commented. "It's a good thing you like raw oysters."

"Right," Stephanie mumbled. "You know, I sure am thirsty."

She reached for her cola. *At least I can drink a lot,* she thought. *And then maybe Jordan won't notice that I can't eat my food!*

"Oh, no!" She accidentally knocked over her glass. A stream of cola spilled over the table. Most of it poured into her lap. The rest of it puddled onto her plate of raw oysters.

"Your food!" Jordan reached across the table for her plate.

Stephanie jumped up from her chair. "Don't worry about it. I wasn't that hungry, anyway." She began to dab at her pants with a napkin.

Oh, this is really sophisticated, she thought. *Spilling soda all over myself.*

Jordan looked at her and shook his head. "This lunch is really turning into a disaster," he said.

"Tell me about it," Stephanie muttered.

She was totally mortified. "I—I think I'd better go to the ladies' room and try to clean up," she said. "But you should go on and eat."

"I don't think so," he said.

Her heart sank. "What do you mean?" she asked. Was Jordan dumping her because she was such a klutz?

"This lunch just isn't working," he said. "Why don't you go clean up. And then we'll talk."

Stephanie felt her heart pound. What did he want to talk about? She hurried toward the ladies' room.

I'm not cool enough for him, she thought miserably. *He's seen through my act. I knew I couldn't pull off being Sabrina! Now he's going to tell me to get lost!*

She felt tears coming to her eyes and blinked them back. Jordan Daniels was one of the nicest, most exciting guys she'd ever met. And she'd spent her one day with him being a total fake!

Chapter
11

Michelle! Over here!" Kaye's voice rang out across the doll department.

"Hey, Kaye," Michelle called as she hurried over to her friend. "Sorry I was gone so long."

"That's all right," Kaye said. "Who paged you, anyway?"

"My sister," Michelle replied. "She reminded me to be back at the hotel by four o'clock to meet my dad."

"No problem," Kaye said.

Michelle stared at the display of Kerrie Dolls. There were Kerries wearing designer outfits. Kerries dressed as astronauts, deep-sea divers, chefs, brides, artists, rock stars, fire fighters, and doctors.

"This is awesome," Michelle said. "I didn't know there was a skateboarder Kerrie!"

Kaye picked up one of the larger boxes. "I want one of these designer Kerries," she said. "Look, this one is wearing a cashmere coat, a silk scarf, and a hand-knit sweater. I wonder if my parents will buy it for me."

Michelle looked at the price tag in disbelief. "That doll costs over three hundred dollars!"

"Well, they're real designer clothes," Kaye said.

Michelle shook her head. "My dad would think I'd lost my mind if I asked for any toy that expensive."

"A Kerrie isn't just a toy," Kaye explained. "It's a collectible. It might be worth a lot more money someday."

Kaye put the doll back on the shelf. "My mother wouldn't buy it, either," she admitted. "But I like to pretend that she would. So what do you want to do now?"

Michelle gazed around the gigantic store.

There wasn't much in FAO Schwarz that she could afford to buy.

"Well, what else is there to do?" Michelle replied. "I mean, it's not like we can go to the zoo or the Empire State Building or anything."

"Is that where you want to go?" Kaye asked.

"Sure," Michelle said. "They're tops on my list of places to see in New York."

Kaye gave her a strange grin. "Perfect! Because that's where *we're* going," she declared.

"Where?" Michelle asked, feeling confused.

"To the Empire State Building," Kaye replied.

"Huh? How could we do that?" Michelle asked.

"Simple," Kaye replied. "We just go."

"But we didn't plan to go there," Michelle said uneasily. She had promised Stephanie she wouldn't change plans again.

"So what? The Empire State Building is awesome," Kaye announced. "You want to see the new Skyride, don't you? It's so cool. It's a movie that makes you feel like you're flying over New York City."

"Of course I want to do that," Michelle said. "But how can—"

"We'll have such a good time," Kaye said.

"Was this your mother's idea?" Michelle asked.

"It's *my* idea." Kaye folded her arms across her chest. "And it's perfectly fine with my parents. I asked them when you answered that page."

"Really?" Michelle felt better.

"I told you," Kaye said, "my parents let me do whatever I want. Besides, my mom said we *have* to go. Because she's meeting us there later."

"She said that?" Michelle asked. She tried to imagine Mrs. Bloom telling Kaye she could go out on her own. "Are you sure?"

"I said so, didn't I?" Kaye snapped.

"Okay, okay. You don't have to get angry about it," Michelle said.

Kaye is so touchy! Michelle thought. But if her mother said they *had* to go to the Empire State Building, then she *had* to go.

"Just let me call my sister first," Michelle said. "I need to tell her my plans have changed."

Kaye followed Michelle as she wound through the store to a pay phone.

Stephanie will be proud of me for being so responsible, Michelle thought. *After all, it's not my fault the plans have changed.*

Besides, Michelle had promised Stephanie that she would stay with the Blooms—and that was what she was doing. The Blooms were the ones who changed the plans. Now they expected her to go to the Empire State Building.

Yeah, Michelle thought, *I am definitely doing the right thing!*

Michelle dialed the hotel and left Stephanie a new message, explaining everything.

"Make sure you tell Stephanie I *had* to change the plans," Michelle repeated to the hotel operator. "She told me I have to stay with the Blooms. And the Blooms are going to the Empire State Building."

Michelle smiled as she hung up the phone. FAO Schwarz *and* the Empire State Building—all in one day! It was too good to be true!

"Okay, let's get going," Kaye told her. She

pulled Michelle out of the store and onto Fifth Avenue. They began walking.

"You know something funny?" Michelle said. "I told my friends Cassie and Mandy I'd be strolling down Fifth Avenue. And here I am!"

"Yeah. It's cool, isn't it?" Kaye asked.

"Even better than I imagined," Michelle said. She had to shout because the street was so loud with the sounds of traffic, sirens, horns, and voices.

Michelle couldn't believe the number of people on Fifth Avenue. There were people in torn jeans, others in luxurious fur coats, others carrying briefcases. Everyone seemed to be taller than they were. And they were all walking very fast.

A group of teens stood on one corner, playing drums. In front of a bookstore, a young man played a violin.

"I love being in New York on our own," Kaye said.

"Yeah. Right." Michelle nodded, but she was starting to feel a little funny about it. New York was amazing. Still, it was kind of strange to walk down the bustling city street without someone older along.

Several minutes passed. "Are we going in the right direction?" Michelle asked.

Kaye pointed ahead, down the wide avenue. Michelle recognized the famous silver spire at the top of the Empire State Building.

"Don't you see it?" Kaye asked. "We're walking right toward it. We'll be there in about five minutes."

"Hot pretzels!" called a man with a little silver cart on the corner.

Michelle was getting hungry. She stopped and bought a hot, salty pretzel from the vendor. Several more minutes passed. She glanced at a street sign. "This is Thirty-ninth Street," she said. "What street did you say the Empire State Building is on?"

"I forget the street, okay?" Kaye replied. "But it doesn't matter. We're almost there."

Michelle looked up—and gasped. "Kaye," she said. Her voice was shaking. "The Empire State Building isn't in sight anymore. It's gone! We're lost! Kaye, what did you do?"

Kaye stared up at the skyline. "I didn't

do anything! It has to be around here someplace."

"But it's one of the tallest buildings in the world," Michelle said. "So how come I can't see it? Where did it go?"

"I don't know," Kaye answered. She was beginning to look worried. "We *did* see it. Let's keep walking. Maybe it will come back into view."

Michelle frowned. "I don't see how! I don't think you know where you're going at all."

"Of course I do," Kaye insisted. "I'm *sure* we'll find it again. It's a zillion feet tall! I mean, anyone could find their way to the Empire State Building!"

"Excuse me," a voice behind them asked. "Do you girls need some help?"

Michelle turned and found herself staring at a kindly looking woman holding two little kids by the hand.

"I'm Mrs. Rudner," the woman introduced herself. "I heard you talking about the Empire State Building," she explained. "It's farther down Fifth. You'll be able to see it if you cross the street."

Michelle stared at the busy city traffic.

Cars, huge buses, and bright yellow taxis crowded the wide avenue. She started to step off the curb. A horn blared at her. Someone yelled, "Little girl, get out of the way! You wanna give me an ulcer?"

Startled, Michelle stepped back onto the sidewalk. Now she wasn't sure she *wanted* to cross the street.

"Where are you parents?" Mrs. Rudner asked her.

Michelle hesitated. She knew she shouldn't talk to strangers. But Mrs. Rudner was being kind and helpful. And right now Michelle needed help.

"My dad's at work," Michelle answered. "We're supposed to meet Kaye's parents at the Empire State Building."

"Meet them?" Mrs. Rudner echoed. She sounded horrified. "Don't your parents realize it's not wise for kids to be out on their own in the city?"

"I guess not," Kaye said quickly. "We're from San Francisco."

"Well, then," Mrs. Rudner said. "Why don't you walk along with us? My children and I are going to the Empire State Building, too."

"Really?" Michelle couldn't believe their luck.

"Really," Mrs. Rudner assured her. "We're going to meet my husband. He runs a newsstand there."

"That would be great," Michelle said.

Kaye glared at her, but Michelle ignored her. At least Mrs. Rudner could lead them safely through the traffic.

And she knew where she was going. Kaye sure didn't! In fact, Michelle was sorry she had ever trusted Kaye to find the way there.

"Here we are," Mrs. Rudner announced a short time later. They entered a huge lobby.

Michelle glanced at the gleaming floors and the sparkling silver trim on the walls and ceiling.

"The elevators are this way." Mrs. Rudner led them across the lobby. She nodded to a tall man at the newsstand on the other side of the lobby. "That's my husband," she said. "Will you girls be okay if we leave you now? Where are your parents?"

"They'll be here soon," Kaye told her. She

sounded a little nervous. "Thanks for all your help."

"Well, look for me at the newsstand if you need anything else." Mrs. Rudner and her family walked away.

"We are so lucky she brought us here," Michelle said.

"*I* could have brought us here, too," Kaye grumbled.

"You didn't know where we were," Michelle pointed out. "You lost the whole Empire State Building."

"I did not!" Kaye turned her back on Michelle. "Hey!" she exclaimed. "Look how long the line is to go up to the second floor for the Skyride!"

Michelle whirled around. A long line started at the elevator and snaked outside. Michelle couldn't even see the end of it.

She glanced at her watch. It was almost two-thirty. That line was awfully long. What if they didn't get into the Skyride until three, or three-thirty? She had to be back *in* the hotel by four!

"No way," Michelle said. "Let's just check out the view on the observation deck. We don't have time to wait in this line. Besides, don't we have to meet your parents soon?"

"Whatever," Kaye said.

Michelle ignored Kaye's cranky tone. "So, where are we supposed to meet them, anyway?" she asked.

"Will you quit bugging me about my parents?" Kaye replied.

Michelle suddenly realized that Kaye wasn't nearly as cool as everyone in school thought she was. Kaye could be a lot of fun, but she could also be bossy and cranky.

"Come on, Michelle . . . let's try the Skyride line," Kaye said. "I know it will be worth the wait. You'll love it."

Michelle shook her head. "The line is too long. Let's just find your parents now."

"We can't find them, okay?" Kaye exploded.

Michelle looked at her in surprise. "What do you mean, we can't?"

"Because they aren't meeting us here," Kaye shouted. "They were *never* meeting us here. I made it all up. Okay? We're on our own, Michelle. No one is coming to meet us!"

Chapter
12

Michelle stared at Kaye in shock. "What do you mean, you lied? Your parents *aren't* coming here?"

Kaye stepped away from the busy elevators to a quieter part of the lobby. "That's what I said," she replied. "They're not coming."

"Why not?" Michelle trailed after Kaye. "How could they just leave us all alone in the Empire State Building? Who's supposed to be responsible for us?"

"We are," Kaye answered. "So what? Your dad let you go out on your own," she pointed out. "And you're a year younger than me."

"I'm not out alone," Michelle said. "I mean, I was supposed to be with your parents."

"What are you talking about?" Kaye asked. "That's not true. You were alone when I saw you in the chocolate shop. You were even charging things to your room! And your sister let you come to FAO Schwarz with me."

"With you and your *parents*," Michelle said. "I was allowed to come only because your parents were with us."

"But I thought you were allowed to be on your own." Kaye stared at Michelle. "I thought your sister was in charge."

"She is," Michelle said.

"Well, didn't she say it was okay for you to go wherever you liked?" Kaye asked.

Michelle bit her lip. "Not exactly," she admitted. "I haven't been telling the whole truth," she went on. "Stephanie *did* say I could go to the store with you. But then she came to find me. She was totally upset that I left the hotel."

"I don't get it," Kaye said.

"It was all a big misunderstanding," Michelle explained. "Stephanie didn't mean to give me permission to leave the hotel." She shook her head in frustration. "Oh, forget it. It's a long story."

Kaye looked more and more worried. "I'm really confused, Michelle. The truth is, I was jealous that you got to be on your own. So I made up all that stuff about being allowed to go anywhere." She swallowed hard. "The truth is, I'm not allowed to go *anywhere* alone. My parents will be furious that we left the store."

"I can't believe this," Michelle exclaimed. "Kaye, I don't like being alone in the middle of New York City. I'm scared!"

Kaye nodded. "I'm a little scared, too! I was scared the whole time we were walking over here. And then, when we couldn't see the building, I was more scared than ever."

"We are in *big* trouble," Michelle said. "How are we supposed to get back to the hotel? I don't even know where it is! Do you?"

Kaye shook her head. "I'm not even sure which direction it's in."

"Well, maybe we can take a cab," Michelle

said. "The cabdriver should know where the Windsor is."

"That costs money," Kaye said in a quiet voice.

Michelle checked her belt pack. "I have two dollars and fifty-six cents left," she reported.

Kaye searched through her wallet. "I have a dollar and ten cents. That's not going to be enough for a cab."

"But I thought you had lots of money," Michelle said.

Kaye stared at the floor. "I lied about that, too."

"Terrific," Michelle muttered. She suddenly had an idea. "I know, we can call Stephanie! She'll come get us!"

"Great!" Kaye exclaimed. "I hope she can get here soon."

Michelle found a pay phone and asked the operator to connect her with the Planet Hollywood restaurant.

"Hello? Planet Hollywood," a hostess answered.

Michelle explained that she wanted to page her sister, Stephanie Tanner.

She waited while the hostess made the announcement. A few minutes passed. "I'm sorry," the hostess said. "Nobody answered the page."

"No answer?" Michelle felt a pang of worry. "Wait! Try asking for Sabrina Tanner," she said.

She waited until the hostess came back on the phone again. "Sorry," she said. "Nobody answered to that name, either."

"She didn't?" Michelle sighed. "Well, thanks." She hung up and turned to Kaye.

"She didn't answer," she said. "But I'm sure Stephanie was going for lunch at Planet Hollywood. I know she wouldn't change her plans."

"Try calling the hotel again," Kaye suggested. "Maybe Stephanie left you a message."

Michelle dialed the hotel.

"Oh, hello, Miss Tanner," the desk clerk greeted her. "Yes, you do have a message. From your father. He said he'll be back at three o'clock instead of four."

Michelle looked at her watch and almost

dropped the phone. It was nearly three o'clock already!

"This is a disaster," she told Kaye. "We've got to get back to the hotel—right now!"

"I'm *not* walking there alone," Kaye declared.

"We won't," Michelle promised. "I have a better idea."

Chapter 13

Stephanie's heart was beating hard as she made her way through Planet Hollywood. Jordan sat at their table, going over their check. He looked grim.

He asked for the check! Stephanie realized. *He's going to say he can't possibly be seen with someone so unsophisticated. And I'm going to have to tell him the truth.*

Stephanie took her seat at the table. "Hi," she said. She hoped she didn't sound as nervous as she felt. "Listen," she began. "I'm really sorry about spilling the soda and—"

"Wait a minute," Jordan said. "I've got to

tell you something, and it isn't easy. So please, just let me say it."

Here it comes, Stephanie thought. *The part where he tells me that I've embarrassed him, and he never wants to see me again.*

"I hate Planet Hollywood," Jordan blurted out.

"What?" Stephanie blinked.

Jordan ran his hand through his hair. "This place. It's loud and crowded. It's where New Yorkers take out-of-towners to impress them. And that's really obnoxious. I'm sorry, Sabrina."

Stephanie didn't know what to say.

Jordan gave her a shy smile. "How about if we start over? How would you feel if I took you to my favorite place in New York to eat?"

Stephanie smiled back at him. She was so relieved she felt like doing a cartwheel. Jordan didn't hate her after all! But Sabrina wouldn't do cartwheels, she reminded herself. "Sure," she said. "That would be fine."

Twenty minutes later, Stephanie and Jordan leaned against the stone wall at Rockefeller Plaza. They were eating hot dogs smothered in mustard and sauerkraut.

Although the November weather was sunny, the ice rink below them was frozen over. Stephanie watched a skater glide gracefully across the ice.

This is the perfect place to eat lunch, she thought. *A real New York experience.*

"I bet you've been here dozens of times," Jordan said.

"No—" *It was getting tiresome being Sabrina,* Stephanie thought. "Only once," she said. "But it's great here. And the hot dog is delicious."

"Glad you like it," Jordan replied. "I wasn't really sure you'd want to grab hot dogs from a hot dog stand."

"Are you kidding? I love it," Stephanie told him. "And it's a lot better than spilling drinks in Planet Hollywood."

"Don't worry about it." Jordan grinned at her. "I'm having a good time. I'm glad we changed our plans."

Stephanie gasped. "Our plans!" she exclaimed.

"What's wrong?" Jordan asked.

She stood up, panicked. "I told Michelle we'd be at Planet Hollywood. I promised not to change plans."

"Does it matter?" Jordan asked.

"I don't know," Stephanie said. "Maybe I'd better call her, just to make sure. She and the Blooms should be back at the hotel by now."

Stephanie hurried to the nearest pay phone and called the hotel.

"Hello, Miss Tanner," the desk clerk said. "This is funny . . . your sister just called a little while ago."

"Michelle called?" Stephanie asked. "What for?"

"She left you a message," the clerk replied. "She said she had to change her plans. She had to stay with the Blooms. And the Blooms went to the Empire State Building."

"What?" Stephanie nearly shouted into the phone.

"I'm sorry," the clerk said.

"Oh, it's not your fault," Stephanie told him. "I just didn't expect anyone to change plans again. But I guess it's okay, as long as Michelle is with the Blooms."

"Wait, Miss Tanner," the clerk said. "I just noticed another message in your mailbox. The other desk clerk must have taken it. Would you like me to read it to you?"

"Yes, please," Stephanie said.

"This message is from Mr. Tanner. He says that he'll be back at the hotel at *three* o'clock instead of four."

Stephanie gasped. "Three?" she exclaimed. "But it's almost three now. Are you sure that's what he said?"

"Yes, miss. I'm positive," the clerk replied. "Would you like to leave another message?"

"No. Thanks." Stephanie hung up and marched back to Jordan. "Jordan, our plans just changed," she said. "We have to go to the Empire State Building. Right this second!"

Jordan stared at her as if she were crazy. "Well, okay," he said. "We'd better grab a cab."

They raced out to the street, and Jordan hailed a yellow cab.

"To the Empire State Building!" Stephanie told the driver as she and Jordan leapt into the backseat.

121

"Okay, Sabrina, what's going on?" Jordan asked.

"It's a long story." Stephanie leaned back and exhaled. "You see, Michelle went to the Empire State Building with the Blooms."

Jordan seemed confused. "What's the big deal about that?" he asked.

"It's just that my dad left a message that he's going to be back at the hotel at three," Stephanie explained. "And it's almost three now."

"Can't you just leave him a message that Michelle might be late?" Jordan asked.

"No. You don't understand! I . . . Michelle . . . we—" Stephanie stopped. It was no use. She couldn't keep up her act anymore. It was just too hard.

"Look, Jordan," she finally said. "I haven't been totally honest with you. Michelle and I were supposed to stay—together—in the hotel all day today," she admitted. "I promised my dad we wouldn't leave."

"Then, why did you leave?"

"It's all pretty confusing," Stephanie said. "I thought Michelle was asking me to go to the game room in the hotel. I didn't realize she was going out with the Blooms—not until I got a message from her later. That's why I said we had to go to FAO Schwarz. I was worried about her."

Jordan's eyebrows arched. "Wow, Sabrina," he said. "Your life is way more complicated than mine."

Stephanie felt her face turning red. "Um, actually, Jordan, I have *another* confession to make. The truth is, I'm not cool at all!" she blurted out. "I've never been to New York before." She took a deep breath. "And—and my name isn't Sabrina. It's Stephanie."

"Huh?" Jordan looked more confused than ever. "Why did you say your name was Sabrina?"

"I was trying to fit in. I wanted you to think I was cool, because *you're* so cool," Stephanie explained. "And I wanted you to think I was on my own. The truth is, if my dad finds out I left the hotel, he'll punish me for all eternity!"

Jordan was absolutely silent.

Stephanie felt her heart pounding. "Well? Do you totally hate me for lying to you?"

Jordan grinned. "Not exactly," he said. "You see—"

The cab pulled over to the curb and stopped. "Empire State Building," the driver announced.

Stephanie paid and slid out of the cab. She stopped for a second and gazed up at the Empire State Building. She had to tilt her head back to see the top.

"It's a hundred and two stories tall," Jordan told her. He pointed toward two rectangular skyscrapers in the distance. "Now the twin towers of the World Trade Center are taller, but for years the Empire State was the tallest building in the world. My dad said that the spire was originally built as a place to anchor giant blimps."

"I never knew that!" Stephanie exclaimed.

"Yup. It never worked out, though," Jordan said. "But there was a radio antenna up there for a while."

Stephanie took one last glimpse at the outside of the building, then glanced at her watch. "We'd better hurry," she said. "We don't have much time."

She rushed up to a doorman. "Excuse me,"

she called. "Have you seen my little sister? She has blond hair and—"

"Are you kidding?" the man interrupted. "I've seen a thousand kids today. I can't remember any of them."

"Forget this," Jordan told her. "We'll look for her ourselves. Let's go."

Jordan led her through the lobby. They grabbed an elevator to the observation deck on the eighty-sixth floor. Stephanie barely glanced at the incredible view of the entire city through the wide glass windows. Instead, she scanned the crowd for her sister.

"Michelle's not here!" she moaned. "Jordan, what will I do? I'm about to be grounded for the rest of my life!"

"Maybe we should go back to the hotel," Jordan suggested. "Michelle might have already gone back there with the Blooms."

"I guess we have no other choice," Stephanie said. She turned back to the elevators. "Oh, no!" she exclaimed. The line to get downstairs was about a block long. "We'll never make it back to the hotel on time!"

"Listen," Jordan told her, "I know a shortcut! We can take the service elevator to the fifty-eighth floor. We can grab an express elevator to the lobby from there. Come on!"

Stephanie followed Jordan as he hurried through a swinging door and down a long hallway. The service elevator was waiting . . . with no other people in sight.

"This is fantastic!" Stephanie exclaimed. "How did you know about this, anyway?"

"My father had a shoot here once," Jordan explained. "I helped him load all his equipment into this same elevator."

Stephanie was impressed. "It's so cool your dad's a famous movie director," she said.

"Oh, yeah." Jordan stared at the floor. "Stephanie, I have something to confess to you, too."

"You do?" Stephanie asked.

"Yeah. I wasn't exactly honest with you, either." Jordan swallowed nervously. "I mean, I *have* met a lot of famous people . . . but only for a second or two. My father isn't a big-time director. Actually, he's . . . an animal trainer. He trains dogs and cats and birds for movies and TV commercials and stuff."

"You're kidding," Stephanie said.

Jordan looked really embarrassed.

Stephanie began to giggle. "Don't feel bad, Jordan," she said. "Because my father isn't a famous TV star, either."

"He isn't?" Jordan looked surprised.

"No," Stephanie said. "He's the host of a morning show. A local talk show. Mostly he interviews people who try to improve the community. It's hardly high-glamour."

Jordan grinned. "Hey, that's pretty cool, actually."

"I guess so." Stephanie grinned back at Jordan. "You know, I don't care what your dad does," she said. "Though I think being an animal trainer sounds pretty amazing!"

"It is," Jordan said. "Hey, did you ever see that bologna commercial with those twin puppies?"

Stephanie nodded. "Sure! They are so cute! I love the way one opens the refrigerator door and the other one takes out the bologna."

"That's Patches and Wiggles," Jordan told her. "My dad trained them. He also trained the birds in the last Lee McMasters movie.

And last week he trained a seal that appeared on *The Lily O'Connor Show*."

"I wish you'd told me all this in the first place," Stephanie said.

"I was afraid 'Sabrina' would think it was boring," Jordan admitted. "To tell you the truth, I'm a lot more comfortable with the real you. Sabrina didn't really seem to like anything. She was a little *too* hip for me."

"You have no idea!" Stephanie told Jordan how she really felt about ordering raw oysters for lunch. "I was pretty relieved when I spilled my drink all over them," she admitted.

Jordan burst out laughing.

The elevator reached the lobby. Stephanie glanced at her watch. "Yikes! It's nearly three!" she exclaimed. "We have exactly five minutes to get back to the hotel—and save my life!"

Chapter
14

Stephanie flew through the hotel's revolving doors. Jordan was right behind her. Stephanie scanned the Windsor's lobby.

"Michelle isn't here!" she exclaimed.

Jordan nodded toward the front desk. "Let's ask the desk clerk if he's seen her."

Stephanie rushed up to the desk. Mrs. Bloom leaned against it, yelling angrily at the clerk.

"Mrs. Bloom!" Stephanie sighed with relief. "I'm so glad you're here! Is Michelle up in our room?"

Mrs. Bloom spun around. "Who are you?" she demanded.

"I'm Stephanie Tanner," Stephanie said. "We met in the laser tag room. You were looking for Kaye, remember? And I was looking for Michelle, my sister."

Mrs. Bloom's eyes opened wide with anger. "Well, Stephanie, your sister is *not* in your room. Your sister is missing. So is my daughter. And it's all Michelle's fault!"

"What are you talking about?" Stephanie asked. "Michelle left me a message. She said she went to the Empire State Building with you!"

"The Empire State Building? I haven't been anywhere near the Empire State Building!" Mrs. Bloom fumed. "I haven't seen Kaye or Michelle since I saw *you* at FAO Schwarz."

"But that was *hours* ago," Stephanie said in surprise.

"I know that," Mrs. Bloom snapped. "My husband and I are absolutely frantic!"

Stephanie shook her head in confusion. "But why would Michelle say she was going with you, when—"

"Kaye!" Mrs. Bloom interrupted, shrieking. "Kaye! You're safe! Thank goodness!"

Jordan tapped Stephanie on the shoulder. "Look!" he cried, pointing behind her.

Stephanie whirled around. *"Michelle!"* she cried. "Where have you been?"

Michelle and Kaye slowly approached the desk.

"Oh, Kaye, my *baby!* I'm so glad you're back!" Mrs. Bloom wrapped her arms around Kaye and gave her a tight hug. "Where have you been? I was worried sick!"

"Yeah, Michelle," Stephanie added. "What happened? Jordan and I went to the Empire State Building like you said. But we couldn't find you anywhere."

"The Empire State Building! They went there? The two of them? Alone?" Mrs. Bloom turned to Stephanie in shock. "Why did they do that? Did you tell them to go?"

"No! I had nothing to do with it," Stephanie protested.

"Then why did they leave FAO Schwarz?" Mrs. Bloom demanded.

"I don't know," Stephanie said. "They were supposed to come back to the hotel with you and Mr. Bloom."

"But Mr. Bloom is still in the store, trying to find them!" Mrs. Bloom said. She turned angrily to Michelle.

"This is your fault, isn't it? How could you do this?" she demanded. "How could you take Kaye to a strange place without telling me?"

"I thought Kaye told you," Michelle said. She turned to her sister. "And I paged you at Planet Hollywood."

"You did?" Stephanie frowned. "I never heard a page."

"I paged you—and Sabrina," Michelle insisted.

Stephanie felt her cheeks flush in embarrassment. "Well, I never heard it," she said. "Unless—" She suddenly groaned. "Unless you paged me when I was in the ladies' room, wiping up this big spill."

"I bet that's what happened!" Michelle declared.

"I'm sorry, Michelle," Stephanie apologized. "I didn't know. And that's when I called the hotel and got the message that Dad would be back early."

"Yeah, I heard that message from Dad, too," Michelle said. "That's why Kaye and I came right back here."

"And how did you get here?" Mrs. Bloom demanded.

"We met this really nice family," Michelle explained. "The Rudners. Mrs. Rudner told us to ask her if we needed help. So we did. She even brought us back here in a cab."

"I don't believe it," Mrs. Bloom murmured. "You should never have been out on your own, taking cabs and talking to strangers. Even if they *were* nice and helpful!"

"That's exactly what Mrs. Rudner told us," Michelle admitted. "I told her it was all a terrible mistake. She said kids should never take on more responsibility than they can handle."

"She was right about that," Stephanie put in.

"Don't worry," Michelle told her. "I agree. And I won't ever do it again!"

Stephanie gave Michelle a hug. "It's okay, Michelle. The important thing is that you're safe. I'm just glad we both made it back here before Dad found out—"

"Found out what?" Their father's voice rang out behind them.

Ulp! Stephanie swallowed hard. *When did Dad get here?* she wondered. She glanced at Jordan.

I'll see you later, he mouthed silently. Stephanie nodded to him and Jordan slipped away.

Then Stephanie turned around. Danny stood behind her, his arms folded over his chest.

"Well, Stephanie?" Danny said. "Why are you and Michelle in the lobby with your jackets on?"

"Dad! Hi!" Stephanie replied. "Um, how was work?" She flashed a big smile.

Danny frowned. "You didn't answer my question," he said. "I want to know what you're doing in the lobby with your jackets on."

Michelle and Stephanie exchanged nervous looks.

"We were cold?" Michelle joked.

"We just wanted to be ready to go out,"

Stephanie said. "In case *you* wanted to go out, that is."

Mrs. Bloom interrupted. "They probably won't ever tell you the truth," she told Danny. "But I'll tell you this—I never want your girls to hang around with my Kaye again. You should punish them good for all of this!"

Mrs. Bloom dragged Kaye over to the desk clerk. Stephanie heard her ask him to get FAO Schwarz on the phone.

"Punish you for what?" Danny asked. "Who was that? And what was she talking about?"

"That was Mrs. Bloom," Stephanie said. "She's from San Francisco, too. Michelle knows her daughter Kaye."

"Really?" Danny's stern expression didn't change. "That's very nice, Stephanie. But you still haven't explained what she meant. And you haven't told me where you both were today," he added.

"Well, I was in the game room for a while," Michelle said.

"Uh-huh." Danny nodded.

"And I went to this really fun fifties snack bar in the hotel," Stephanie chimed in.

"I thought you had lunch in the dining room," Danny said. "With the Blooms."

Stephanie gulped. "You did?"

"That's what I said in my message," Michelle explained.

"I didn't know you left Dad that message," Stephanie said.

"I didn't know *you* left a message that said we'd be in the game room," Michelle replied.

"Oh. Well, see, Dad—" Stephanie turned to their father—"I think I can explain everything—"

"Oh, you *both* have plenty of explaining to do," Danny said. "But right now I want you to march into the elevator and go up to your room. I'm going to speak with Mrs. Bloom. Then I'll come up—and we'll get to the bottom of all this."

Stephanie and Michelle walked slowly to the elevator.

"Do you think Dad is really mad?" Michelle asked.

"Yes," Stephanie replied.

"Well, he always gets over it," Michelle said.

"Eventually," Stephanie agreed. "But I have a feeling that our New York vacation just came to an end."

Chapter
15

Stephanie flopped onto her king-size bed. "That scene in the lobby was awful," she said.

"The worst," Michelle agreed. She sat on the edge of the bed next to Stephanie. "But I was telling the truth, Steph. It really wasn't my idea to leave Kaye's parents and go to the Empire State Building alone. It really wasn't."

"I believe you," Stephanie assured her.

"It's not fair that Mrs. Bloom thinks it was all my fault," Michelle went on. "Kaye promised that her parents would meet us there."

"Maybe you can explain everything to them sometime," Stephanie offered.

"I don't think so," Michelle said. "I don't think Kaye or her parents will ever speak to me again."

Stephanie sighed. It had been a long, strange day. She suddenly realized how tired she was.

"This day didn't turn out anything like I imagined," she told Michelle.

"Yeah," Michelle said. "I never thought I'd get to play laser tag. Or go to the Empire State Building alone."

"And I never thought I'd end up at Planet Hollywood." Stephanie grinned. "Some bad stuff happened, but I guess some pretty good stuff happened, too."

There was a knock on the door. "Stephanie? It's Jordan!"

Stephanie leapt up and answered the door. "Hi, Jordan," she said.

"Can you talk for a few minutes?" Jordan asked.

"Only a few," Stephanie replied. "My dad will be up here soon. And he's pretty upset."

"That's what it looked like," Jordan said.

"Still, he seemed much calmer than *my* dad."
Jordan grinned. "My dad would have been
yelling and screaming."

Stephanie grinned back. Meeting Jordan
was definitely one of the *good* things that
happened.

"Anyway, I wanted to say that I really had
fun hanging out with you," Jordan added.
"And I have a surprise, too."

"Tickets to *The Lily O'Connor Show?*" Michelle piped up.

"Michelle!" Stephanie exclaimed.

Jordan blushed. "No. I couldn't get those,"
he admitted. "But my dad said you and Michelle could come to his shoot tomorrow
morning."

"Jordan's dad trains animals for TV commercials," Stephanie explained to her sister.

"I'd love to see that!" Michelle exclaimed.

"So would I," Stephanie said. "If my dad
doesn't ground us for life, that is!"

Jordan laughed. "There won't be any celebrities there or anything, but it should be
fun."

"Will there be any famous animals?" Michelle asked.

"Sort of," Jordan said. "Have you ever heard of Ling-Ling and Tsing-Tsing?"

"The Chinese *pandas!*" Michelle squealed in excitement. "I can't believe it! They're totally famous. I promised my class I'd take their picture at the zoo!"

"Really? How would you like to take a special, personal picture with them?" Jordan asked.

"That would be fabulous!" Michelle answered. "That would make this the absolute best trip of my whole life!"

"That sounds great, Jordan," Stephanie told him. "Thanks so much for asking us."

"No problem," Jordan said. "I'll call you tonight to set it up. And to make sure it's okay with your dad."

"Thanks!" Stephanie waved to him as he stepped onto the elevator.

Then she closed the door behind her and sat back down next to Michelle.

"Do you think Dad's too mad to let us go?" Michelle asked.

"I hope not," Stephanie said. "Let's just hope he's in a forgiving mood. A *very* forgiving mood."

The door swung open and Danny stepped into the room. He pulled the desk chair up next to the bed and sat down facing them.

"Dad, we're really sorry!" Stephanie blurted out before he could say a word.

"Really, *really* sorry," Michelle added. "It's all my fault. Stephanie only left the hotel because she was looking for me."

"Well, Michelle only left because she bumped into Kaye in the chocolate shop," Stephanie explained.

"Right. And Kaye's the one who asked if I wanted to go to FAO Schwarz," Michelle said.

"And Michelle asked if she could go, which was very responsible of her," Stephanie added. "But I was in the shower washing my hair. So when Michelle said *Kaye Bloom*, I thought she said *game room*."

Danny shook his head. "Wait a minute! I—"

"Wait, Dad," Stephanie begged. "Please let us finish! Then I met Jordan, and we asked the doorman, and the doorman said Michelle took a taxi to FAO Schwarz with a family. So Jordan took me over there to look for her."

Danny looked bewildered. "Who is Jordan?" he asked.

"He's the one who asked us to meet Ling-Ling and Tsing-Tsing on Saturday," Michelle replied.

"The Chinese pandas," Stephanie explained. "Jordan's father is an animal trainer."

"I'm lost," Danny said.

"But it's all totally simple," Stephanie told him. "You see, we found Michelle, but she said she was staying at the toy store with the Blooms. And that's the only reason I went to Planet Hollywood with Jordan."

"But Kaye tricked me," Michelle went on. "Because she's the one who said her parents were going to meet us at the Empire State Building. But they weren't! So it's all Kaye's fault, really."

"Now, hold on," Danny said. "I just want to know why—"

"Why I went to the Empire State Building?" Stephanie interrupted. "Because I got *your* message that you were coming back early. So Jordan and I had to find Michelle."

143

"Girls, wait," Danny said. "I'm trying to tell you that—"

There was another knock on the door.

Stephanie and Michelle exchanged puzzled looks.

"Who could that be?" Stephanie asked.

Danny opened the door. The Blooms stood in the hallway. "We came to apologize," Mrs. Bloom said.

"I told my parents that it was my fault," Kaye told Michelle. "I thought Michelle was allowed to go around on her own. So I tricked her into going off without my parents."

"We're very sorry," Mr. Bloom told Danny. "We're just glad everyone is back safe and sound."

"Wait a minute!" Danny held up his hands. "Will everyone stop apologizing to everyone else?"

The Blooms stared at him in surprise.

"I mean, it's very nice that you *want* to apologize," Danny said. "But I can see that there were a lot of misunderstandings going on."

He turned to Stephanie and Michelle.

"This is why I told you to stay put in the first place," he said. "I know how easy it is to get plans confused."

"Now we know it, too," Stephanie agreed.

Kaye pulled Michelle aside. "Listen, I promise not to tell anyone at school what happened."

"I won't if you won't," Michelle agreed. "See you in a few days," she called as the Blooms left the room.

Danny sighed. "You girls had one crazy day," he said. "I don't know if I'll ever understand exactly what happened."

Stephanie and Michelle were silent.

"I have a phone call to make," Danny went on. "I want you both to think about what you did today. I'll let you know your punishment when I get back."

Danny strode into his room. He closed the adjoining door.

Stephanie sighed. "I guess we can forget about going to the commercial shoot," she said.

"And I guess I can forget about being allowed anywhere on my own," Michelle said.

A few minutes later Danny returned to their room.

"I'm still very upset that you didn't listen to me today," he told them. "But I can see that in some ways you *were* trying to be responsible."

"We really were," Michelle said.

Danny frowned. "But you also twisted my words around."

"I know," Michelle whispered.

"I make rules for a reason," Danny went on. "And I want you to follow them. If I say stay together, you stay together."

"We will, Dad," Stephanie promised. "We'll really listen from now on."

Michelle nodded in agreement. "I'll try a lot harder," she said.

"Okay. I only hope you both learned a lesson from all this," Danny told them.

"I did!" Michelle exclaimed. "I was really scared when Kaye and I were alone. I'm not ready for that yet."

"Yeah. And I felt terrible when I couldn't find Michelle," Stephanie added.

"Now you know how *I* feel sometimes," Danny said. "But I've decided that what you've been through today is enough punishment for now.''

Stephanie's mouth dropped open. ''You mean . . . we're not grounded for life?''

''Not yet.'' Danny smiled and shook his head. ''We'll work something out when we get home. But I don't want to punish anybody while we're all on vacation.''

Stephanie and Michelle exchanged glances.

''Really, Dad?'' Michelle asked.

Danny nodded. ''Especially since I have a huge surprise for you tonight.''

Stephanie's eyes lit up. ''A surprise? What is it?''

Danny grinned. ''Well, there's a reason I wanted to get back here early.'' He paused. ''Because I have the last three tickets for tonight's taping of *The Lily O'Connor Show!*''

Stephanie and Michelle both screamed at the same time.

''I know how much you like the show,'' Danny added. ''So I asked my producer if he could get us tickets, and he did.''

''That is so great!'' Michelle said.

''Totally!'' Stephanie agreed. ''Darcy and Allie will be able to see us on TV after all!''

Danny smiled. "Good. And I promise to do whatever you girls want for the rest of our trip."

"Excellent!" Stephanie said. "Can we go to the Hard Rock Cafe? And then shopping at Bloomingdale's?"

"But I want to take a boat ride around the city," Michelle said. "And go in-line skating in Central Park."

"In-line skating?" Stephanie glanced at Michelle impatiently. "We do that all the time at home."

"Well, it's more fun than *shopping*," Michelle argued.

Stephanie's expression brightened. "Hey, I know!" she said. "Why don't we split up and—" She stopped. "Ooops! Did I just say that?"

She looked at Michelle. Michelle looked at Danny.

He laughed. "Well, I guess I can't expect sisters to agree on everything," he said. "So there's only one solution to this problem."

"Oh, no. Do we have to do what Stephanie wants because she's older?" Michelle asked.

"No," Danny said. "I promised we'd do what you *both* want. So we'll just have to do *everything*—together."

"That's okay, Dad," Stephanie told him. "Doing things together is what we like best of all!"

FULL HOUSE Stephanie™

PHONE CALL FROM A FLAMINGO	88004-7/$3.99
THE BOY-OH-BOY NEXT DOOR	88121-3/$3.99
TWIN TROUBLES	88290-2/$3.99
HIP HOP TILL YOU DROP	88291-0/$3.99
HERE COMES THE BRAND NEW ME	89858-2/$3.99
THE SECRET'S OUT	89859-0/$3.99
DADDY'S NOT-SO-LITTLE GIRL	89860-4/$3.99
P.S. FRIENDS FOREVER	89861-2/$3.99
GETTING EVEN WITH THE FLAMINGOES	52273-6/$3.99
THE DUDE OF MY DREAMS	52274-4/$3.99
BACK-TO-SCHOOL COOL	52275-2/$3.99
PICTURE ME FAMOUS	52276-0/$3.99
TWO-FOR-ONE CHRISTMAS FUN	53546-3/$3.99
THE BIG FIX-UP MIX-UP	53547-1/$3.99
TEN WAYS TO WRECK A DATE	53548-X/$3.99
WISH UPON A VCR	53549-8/$3.99
DOUBLES OR NOTHING	56841-8/$3.99
SUGAR AND SPICE ADVICE	56842-6/$3.99
NEVER TRUST A FLAMINGO	56843-4/$3.99
THE TRUTH ABOUT BOYS	00361-5/$3.99
CRAZY ABOUT THE FUTURE	00362-3/$3.99
MY SECRET ADMIRER	00363-1/$3.99
BLUE RIBBON CHRISTMAS	00830-7/$3.99
THE STORY ON OLDER BOYS	00831-5/$3.99
MY THREE WEEKS AS A SPY	00832-3/$3.99
NO BUSINESS LIKE SHOW BUSINESS	01725-X/$3.99

Available from Minstrel® Books Published by Pocket Books

FULL HOUSE™
Michelle

#5: THE GHOST IN MY CLOSET 53573-0/$3.99

#6: BALLET SURPRISE 53574-9/$3.99

#7: MAJOR LEAGUE TROUBLE 53575-7/$3.99

#8: MY FOURTH-GRADE MESS 53576-5/$3.99

#9: BUNK 3, TEDDY, AND ME 56834-5/$3.99

#10: MY BEST FRIEND IS A MOVIE STAR!
(Super Edition) 56835-3/$3.99

#11: THE BIG TURKEY ESCAPE 56836-1/$3.99

#12: THE SUBSTITUTE TEACHER 00364-X/$3.99

#13: CALLING ALL PLANETS 00365-8/$3.99

#14: I'VE GOT A SECRET 00366-6/$3.99

#15: HOW TO BE COOL 00833-1/$3.99

#16: THE NOT-SO-GREAT OUTDOORS 00835-8/$3.99

#17: MY HO-HO-HORRIBLE CHRISTMAS 00836-6/$3.99

MY AWESOME HOLIDAY FRIENDSHIP BOOK
(An Activity Book) 00840-4/$3.99

FULL HOUSE MICHELLE OMNIBUS 02181-8/$6.99

#18: MY ALMOST PERFECT PLAN 00837-4/$3.99

#19: APRIL FOOLS 01729-2/$3.99

A MINSTREL® BOOK
Published by Pocket Books

Simon & Schuster Mail Order Dept. BWB
200 Old Tappan Rd., Old Tappan, N.J. 07675

Please send me the books I have checked above. I am enclosing $_____ (please add $0.75 to cover the
postage and handling for each order. Please add appropriate sales tax). Send check or money order--no cash or C.O.D.'s please. Allow up to
six weeks for delivery. For purchase over $10.00 you may use VISA: card number, expiration date and customer signature must be included.

Name _____

Address _____

City _____ State/Zip _____

VISA Card # _____ Exp.Date _____

Signature _____

1033-26